SUMMER WEDDINGS

A season of confetti and whirlwind romances!

You are cordially invited to attend the
Huntingdon-Cross summer weddings.

Celebrate the shotgun marriage of
Daisy Huntingdon-Cross and Sebastian Beresford
in
Expecting the Earl's Baby
by Jessica Gilmore
Save the date: on sale April 2015

Raise a glass to Rose Huntingdon-Cross
and Will Carter as they finally tie the knot
in
A Bride for the Runaway Groom
by Scarlet Wilson
Save the date: on sale May 2015

Join us in celebrating Violet Huntingdon-Cross
and Tom Buckley's star-studded wedding day
in
Falling for the Bridesmaid
by Sophie Pembroke
Save the date: on sale June 2015

Dear Reader,

When I was asked if I'd like to take part in a collaboration for a trilogy, I think I said yes before I'd even learned that the theme for the three books was one of my absolute favourites—*Summer Weddings*!

As much as I always enjoy myself, planning and writing my books, Tom and Violet's story was even more fun than usual. Firstly I got to work with two of my favourite writers and lovely people Scarlet Wilson and Jessica Gilmore. Through phone calls, Skype, and endless emails we built a family and a world together. And then—best of all—we got to sit out in the sunshine together at a conference and hammer out the details and all the fun bits that made the series come alive for us.

Writing the third part of a trilogy comes with some responsibility, though, and my biggest concern before I started work on the book was living up to the two stories that came before it. But once I'd read them I realised that everything I needed was already there—all that was left was to finish the story my friends had started.

I hope I did them justice, and that you have as much fun reading Tom and Violet's story (as well as Daisy and Seb's and Rose and Will's) as we had coming up with them.

Love and confetti!

Sophie

FALLING FOR
THE BRIDESMAID

BY
SOPHIE PEMBROKE

First published in Great Britain 2015
by Mills & Boon, an imprint of Harlequin (UK) Limited,
Eton House, 18-24 Paradise Road, Richmond, Surrey, TW9 1SR

© 2015 Sophie Pembroke

ISBN: 978-0-263-25817-2

Harlequin (UK) Limited's policy is to use papers that are natural,
renewable and recyclable products and made from wood grown in
sustainable forests. The logging and manufacturing processes conform
to the legal environmental regulations of the country of origin.

Printed and bound in Great Britain
by CPI Antony Rowe, Chippenham, Wiltshire

Sophie Pembroke has been reading and writing romance ever since she read her first Mills & Boon® at university, so getting to write them for a living is a dream come true!

Sophie lives in a little Hertfordshire market town in the UK, with her scientist husband and her incredibly imaginative five-year-old daughter. She writes stories about friends, family and falling in love, usually while drinking too much tea and eating homemade cakes. She also keeps a blog at SophiePembroke.com

Books by Sophie Pembroke

Mills & Boon® Romance

Stranded with the Tycoon
Heiress on the Run
A Groom Worth Waiting For
His Very Convenient Bride

Visit the author profile page at millsandboon.co.uk for more titles

For George and Karen, for making this book possible
through coffee, childcare and cheerleading!
Thank you both, so much.

CHAPTER ONE

THE SWEET SMELL of rose petals filled the evening air, giving the falling dusk a sultry warmth. Music sang out from the band on the patio, romantic with just an undertone of sexy. Fairy lights twinkled in the branches of the trees and inside the marquees, and around them leaves rustled in the still warm breeze.

The whole set-up was so perfectly loved-up Violet thought she might be physically ill if she had to suffer through it a moment longer.

Glaring down at her lavender bridesmaid's dress, she slunk to the edge of the celebrations where she could watch the live band play in peace. She needed to make more of an effort to enjoy the evening, and maybe the music would help. Her parents' vow renewal ceremony had been beautiful, and the party that followed a huge success. Later, she had no doubt, her dad and the boys from The Screaming Lemons would take to the stage and wow the remaining guests all over again, even though they'd finished their official set an hour ago. Knowing Dad, it would probably be a lower key, acoustic set the second time around.

Keeping Dad off the stage was always more trouble than getting him on there, and he always wanted one more encore. But for now the support act seemed to be doing well enough. The courtyard in front of the stage was filled

with people dancing, or just holding each other, or kissing. Falling in love.

Violet scowled and looked away.

Of course, the situation wasn't helped by her family.
There, leaning against her new husband—Lord Sebastian Beresford, Earl of Holgate, if you please—was her
youngest sister, Daisy. No, the Lady Holgate now. Hard
to believe that Daisy-Waisy was an honest-to-God count-
ess, but somehow not quite as impossible to process as the
slight swell of her baby bump under her carefully chosen
emerald-green bridesmaid's dress.

Just a few more months and Violet would officially be
the maiden aunt of the family. Hell, she was already doing
the church flowers most weekends, and taking tea with
her mother's 'ladies who lunch' crowd. Maybe she should
just skip straight ahead to adopting a three-legged cat and
taking up crochet.

Actually, she'd quite like to learn to crochet, but that
wasn't the point.

Seb rested his hand against his wife's stomach, and
Daisy's soft smile grew into a fully fledged grin as she
tilted her face for a kiss. Violet turned away, suddenly em-
barrassed to be staring.

But unfortunately her gaze just landed on Rose and
Will, looking equally wrapped up in each other. Her twin
sister and her best friend. Violet had to admit she really
hadn't seen that one coming either. An attraction, perhaps,
or maybe even a fling. Not that Will would give up his
runaway groom status for good and marry into her family. But there Rose stood in her own wedding dress, after
sneaking away for their own secret marriage ceremony
once their parents' vow renewal service was over.

Maybe she just had no sort of love radar at all. Or maybe
it was broken. That would explain a hell of a lot, really.

Will glanced up at just the wrong moment and, this time, Violet couldn't look away quick enough. Even staring pointedly at the band, she couldn't miss the whispered conversation between Rose and *her* new husband. Probably trying to decide whose responsibility Violet's hurt feelings were now.

Violet sighed. It wasn't that she wasn't happy for her sisters—she really, truly was. And she knew that their happiness shouldn't make her own sorry situation feel so much worse. But it did.

Swallowing, she looked down at her feet, and the high heels pinching her toes. It would pass, she knew. Any day now she'd be able to look at all the happy and loved-up people around her and just smile, without the bitter tinge that threatened to colour her whole world.

That day just wasn't yet, that was all.

'She thinks you're cross with her, you know. Or me, possibly,' Will said, standing beside her with his hands in his pockets. Such a familiar sight at these events. Usually Will's presence was a comfort, a reliable soul to help her through the amused looks, the only half-whispered comments, and the occasional drunken suggestion from guys she barely knew but who clearly thought they knew all about her—and her sexual proclivities.

Today, though, he was just a reminder that things wouldn't ever be the same again.

'Cross with Rose?' Violet asked, mustering up a smile. 'Why on earth would I be cross with her? For stealing you away from me? Good riddance, I say.'

The startled look on Will's face told her she'd misjudged something very badly.

'Uh, no. She thinks you're mad because you got landed with picking up that reporter guy from the airport tonight, so you're missing out on the good champagne. That or the whole Benefit Concert thing.'

Ah, that. Yeah, that would make more sense. Especially since she hadn't been completely silent about her unhappiness that the reporter was coming at all.

'I hadn't really…you think she stole me away from you?'

Violet gave him a withering stare. 'Yes, Will. I've been lusting after you, pining away for you through every one of your ridiculous engagements and runaway groom stunts. And now you've finally married my sister, I don't think I will ever recover.'

Her deadpan delivery apparently sold it because Will laughed with obvious relief. 'Good. That's…okay, then. And you're not mad about the reporter either?'

'I'm mad about the champagne. Otherwise, I'll cope.'

'You're sure? I know you're a little…'

Violet tried to guess the word he was avoiding saying. Nervous? Worried? Paranoid?

Probably paranoid.

'Apprehensive about him coming,' Will finished.

Violet sighed. Apprehensive wasn't the half of it. But her dad had made up his mind that he wanted to tell his story, have that official biography on the shelves, and he'd picked this guy to do it. Rose had looked at her with worried eyes when he'd announced it, but even she admitted it made sense to do it now, ahead of the new tour and album. The reporter guy would have exclusive access, in-depth interviews and enough connections to get a real buzz going in the media.

'Rose says he's nice,' Will tried. 'They met in New York before she came home.'

'I'm sure he's a doll,' Violet replied. It didn't matter who he was. He was press, and only interested in them as a story, as something he could sell.

Violet had learned that lesson the hard way.

Will frowned. 'Maybe if you talk to your dad…'

Shaking her head, Violet gave him a gentle smile. 'It's fine. I promise.' Dad had made up his mind and that was it. As always. Nothing Will, Daisy, Rose or Violet could do to change it. And so there was no point dwelling on it. She'd just stay out of his way as much as possible and hope for the best.

What else could she do?

'And about the Benefit Concert—' he started, but Violet cut him off.

'Go on, Will.' She pushed against his arm. 'Go whisk Rose away on your honeymoon. I'll take care of things here, I promise. Since you've apparently already texted the reporter guy my phone number, he's my responsibility now, and I think I can manage one airport pick-up. You two go relax for a bit. Get used to being married for once, instead of just temporarily engaged.'

'Okay. See you soon, kid.' With a quick hug and a peck on the cheek, he headed back towards Rose, and Violet was alone again.

As usual.

She hadn't exactly *lied* to Will, she decided. She had never thought of Will as husband material—or even one-night stand material. He was worth far more to her as a friend, and she'd never felt that spark, that flash of something more that hinted that they could be anything else.

It was just kind of weird that he obviously felt that flash with *Rose* of all people. Her so-identical-it-was-actually-spooky twin sister.

Although, really, she should be used to people seeing something in Rose that they never saw in her. After all, hadn't their parents made Rose stay home instead of going back to the States after Daisy's wedding, just so she could organise their vow renewal ceremony and party? Even though Violet had been right there, with time on her hands, happy to help?

Not that she was bitter. She knew why they hadn't asked—because they'd been sure she wouldn't want to do it. Wouldn't want to have to deal with so many people, so many knowing eyes.

And they were probably right.

Will hadn't thought about that as he'd told her where to find Rose's black planner, though, and asked her to make sure everything kept ticking over for the annual Huntingdon Hall Benefit Concert while they were away on their honeymoon. Maybe he'd just been too caught up in the flush of true love to think about it. Or maybe he expected her to hand it over to some agency person, hired to cover Rose's job.

Maybe she should. After all, she knew absolutely nothing about how to organise a concert for thousands of people. Will had insisted that Rose had already done all the hard work, that there'd be practically nothing left for Violet to do.

Because obviously otherwise they'd have found someone more competent to put in charge.

Violet shook her head. She was being ridiculous. She hadn't wanted to organise the vow renewal anyway. Or the Benefit Concert, come to that. She had other obligations. But now that Rose had told their dad she'd be stepping down from her job managing the PR and events for The Screaming Lemons once she got back from her honeymoon...well, someone would have to do it. And Violet couldn't ignore the very small part of her brain that thought that person could be her.

No. She had no experience, and no desire to deal with people who laughed at her behind her back all day long.

She'd just stick to things she knew she was good at. Like arranging flowers, thank you very much.

The flower displays she'd designed for the vow renewal were, she decided, by far her best displays yet. Lots of exotic blooms in deep jewel colours. Striking and memorable, just like her parents. Her flowers rocked, everyone said so.

There you had it. Twenty-seven years on the planet, and that was all she could say about herself.

Violet Huntingdon-Cross—kick-ass flower arranger, wannabe crocheter. Potential cat lady in waiting.

No, that wasn't all. That was just all that other people saw—and she was happy to keep it that way. She made a difference in the lives of young people and teenagers every day, even if no one ever knew it was her. After all, if word got around that Violet Huntingdon-Cross was manning the phones at the troubled teen helpline, their calls would skyrocket with people wanting to ask her about her own past, or just talk to a minor celebrity—and the kids she really wanted to help wouldn't be able to get through at all. So she helped where she could. Even if she wished she could do more.

Her parents did the same, helping out charities anonymously when they could. The only difference was, they also did enough charity work—as well as music and the occasional modelling gig respectively—in public that everyone assumed they already knew everything there was to know about Rick and Sherry Cross.

But with Violet…well, Violet could only imagine what they were *still* saying about her. Probably the nicest was that she'd become a recluse.

Still, that was a hell of a lot better than what they'd been saying about her eight years ago.

Pulling her phone from her tiny clutch bag, she checked the time and then double-checked the email Will had sent her from Rose's account with the reporter guy's flight details. Thomas Buckley…that was his name. She must make an effort not to just call him reporter guy all the time. Although it never hurt to have a reminder that the press were press and always on the record, whatever they said. Not something she ever wanted to forget again.

Time to go. She'd get changed out of her bridesmaid's dress, grab the ridiculous name card Rose had left for her and be at Heathrow in plenty of time to grab a coffee before his flight landed. And, best of all, she wouldn't be stuck in romance central another minute.

Moving towards the side door to Huntingdon Hall, Violet paused as she caught sight of her parents, dancing in the light of the just risen moon. So wrapped up in each other that the couple of hundred people watching, who'd come all this way to celebrate with them, might not even be there at all. Sherry Huntingdon and Rick Cross were famously crazy about each other, but it wasn't until Violet caught them in moments like this that she really believed the media hype.

And that, she finally admitted to herself, was the real reason all this love stuff was getting to her. Deep down, she'd always believed that she'd just fall into a perfect relationship like her parents had, like both her sisters had now found too.

Instead, she'd got something else entirely. Like anti-love. The sort of relationship that tore up your insides and made you someone else. After that, if she was honest, Violet wasn't sure she'd ever have the courage to try again.

Her phone rang in her hand and Violet answered it automatically, glad for the distraction. 'Hello?'

'I was under the impression that you, whoever you are, were supposed to be meeting me at the airport about twenty minutes ago.' The American drawl made Violet's eyes widen. The reporter guy. Except Rose's email had him landing in an hour and a half. Dammit!

'I'm so sorry, Mr...' Oh, God, what was his name?

'Buckley.' He bit the surname out. 'And I could care less about apologies. Just get here, will you? I'll be in the bar.'

And, with that, the line went dead.

Picking up her skirt, Violet dashed for the garage and prayed no one had blocked her car in. She'd have to borrow one of her dad's if they had. No time to change now, or even pick up that specially made name card of Rose's. If she ever wanted to be relied on for more than flowers, she needed to not screw this up. And since the bad impression she—and by extension her family—had made on the reporter guy was already done, she needed to find a way to fix it. Starting with getting to Heathrow as fast as humanly possible, *before* he started drafting his story. She knew journalists. The truth seldom got in the way of a good story, and once they thought they knew all about a person it was almost impossible to convince them otherwise.

And Violet had already earned the Huntingdon-Cross family enough bad press to last a lifetime.

CHAPTER TWO

TOM PUSHED HIS way to the counter, dragging his suitcase behind him like a weapon. A coffee shop. What the hell kind of use to him was that, especially at this time of night? He needed a drink—a proper one. But that was arrivals for you—never as good as the departures lounge. After so many years travelling the world, you'd think he'd remember that. Except he was usually being collected straight off a plane these days, and got whisked through arrivals to some hotel or another without even clocking his surroundings.

He'd just have to hope that whoever the ditsy woman Rose had assigned to pick him up was would check her phone and see his text telling her to meet him here instead.

Staring at the menu above the counter with bleary eyes, Tom tried to figure out his best option. He'd already consumed so much caffeine in the last two weeks that his muscles appeared to be permanently twitching. Add that to the distinct lack of sleep, and he wasn't sure another shot of the black stuff was quite what he needed. Of course, what he *needed* was a big bed with cool sheets, a blackout blind and about twenty-four hours' solid rest.

None of which was a remote possibility until his ride pitched up.

Ordering a decaf something-or-other, Tom tossed his

jacket and laptop into the nearest bucket chair and hovered impatiently between it and the counter while he waited for his drink. If he'd flown first class, or even business, he could have had as many free drinks as he liked on the plane. But old habits died hard and, since this job was entirely on spec and therefore on his own dime, he'd been paying for his own flight. Something inside him still baulked at shelling out that much cash just for a better seat, even though money wasn't really an object any more. Certainly not the way it had been growing up.

His music journalism career had taken off enough in the past few years that he could rely on his contacts for a good life and a better income. He'd come a long way from his first big, explosive story, almost ten years ago.

So yeah, he could have afforded the upgrade, easily, and without tapping those savings. And if he'd remembered about the free booze aspect of things, he probably would have done. As it was…

Snatching his coffee from the girl behind the counter, he settled at his table and prepared to hang around a while. God only knew how long it would take his ride to get there from wherever she was, but he might as well get some work done while he waited. Even if he felt as if his eyes might jump right out of his head if he didn't close them soon.

At least the work was worth travelling all the way from New York for. A story like this, a break this big…it could make him, permanently. He'd be the go-to person for anything to do with The Screaming Lemons, and that was serious currency in the industry. It would give him access, and opportunities with the newer bands coming through. He'd have the pick of jobs.

He'd already made a pretty good name for himself with the bigger music magazines, websites and even the colour supplements. But this trip, these interviews, this was something more—it was a book in the making. That was what Rick Cross had promised him. And Tom was going to make sure the old man made good on his word.

He was annoyed to have missed all the upheaval in the Huntingdon-Cross family over the past two months, but it couldn't be helped. He'd already been committed to another project at home in the States and, anyway, who could have predicted that one of Rick and Sherry's famously blonde and beautiful daughters would get married and knocked up all within the space of eight weeks? And who knew what was going on with Rose now? She'd been in the press recently herself, he remembered, pictured with the famous Runaway Groom—who he'd *thought* was famously her sister *Violet's* best friend. Maybe something had happened there—and he'd missed it, again. All *he'd* had was a text message when he turned his phone back on after the flight, with a contact number and the information that, due to unforeseen but brilliant circumstances, someone else would be collecting him.

Or not, as the case might be.

Tom sighed. He'd just have to make sure he got good interviews with them all when he could. And, wherever Rose might be, at least one daughter was still living at home—probably the most famous one, if you counted notorious Internet celebrity, which Tom did.

Opening his laptop, he pulled up his notes on the family. He was staying at the family home, Huntingdon Hall, so he needed to be prepared from the get-go. He'd spent weeks compiling old interviews, articles and photos of the whole family, and felt he had it pretty much down. And after speaking with Rose in New York and on the phone while planning the trip, he'd thought he had at least one ally there—until she'd decided to swan off and abandon him with no notice.

Presumably she'd got an offer too good to refuse, no matter how much it inconvenienced anyone else. Celebrity kids—always the centre of their own world, however nice and normal Rose had seemed when they met. He needed to remember that.

He'd only had one conversation with the man he was really there to see, though—Rick Cross himself. Rock star, family man, reformed wide boy. The interviews Tom had on file dated back almost thirty years, back to when The Screaming Lemons were the next big thing on the rock scene. Nowadays, they were the old standards—and they had to try harder to shock or surprise.

With his plans for a tell-all book about the band and his family's history, it looked as if Rick had plans to do both.

Tom had asked him, 'Why now?' It couldn't be money—the band still sold enough greatest hits records and got more than enough airplay that it didn't matter if their latest album tanked. But all Rick would say was that it was time.

Scrolling through his family crib sheet, Tom reminded himself of all the most pertinent facts.

Most people in Britain and the States could pick Rick Cross out of a line-up and tell you his story. Same for his wife, the beautiful and rich mostly ex-model and now English society stalwart, Sherry Huntingdon. With his fame and her family, they made quite the impact.

Then there were the girls. The youngest, Daisy, was the newest Lady Holgate, which seemed pretty much par for the course for celebrity kids, Tom decided. After all, if you already had money and fame, surely a title was the only thing left to go for? Especially in the UK.

The twins were a few years older at twenty-seven. Rose, he knew from personal meetings with her, had been living in New York for the last few years, although she had planned to be in England until the annual benefit concert at least.

And then there was Violet. Tom had enjoyed the hell out of researching her. The thought made him smile even as he rubbed at his gritty eyes.

A commotion at the counter made him look up, and he blinked at the sight of a tall blonde in a ridiculous dress and heels crashing past a table full of customers. Was that Rose? Or a sleep deprivation induced hallucination?

'Sorry!' the blonde yelped, and he decided that she was probably real. Hallucinations didn't usually yelp, in his experience.

Shaking his head to try and wake up, Tom packed up his laptop. It looked as if his ride had made it after all. Any time now he could fall into that nice, peaceful, quiet bed and sleep for a week. Or at least until Rick Cross summoned him for his first interview.

From all the reports he'd read, Tom was pretty sure Rick wasn't an early riser. That lie-in was practically in the bag.

'Rose,' he said, hoisting his bag onto his shoulder and reaching for the handle of his suitcase. 'I thought you were going away? You didn't have to come all the way out here just because the idiot you asked to pick me up forgot. I could have just caught a cab, you know.'

Rose looked up, eyes wide, her hands still gripping her skirt. 'Oh, um, no, it's fine. Thomas. It's fine, Thomas.'

Why did she keep repeating his name? And why was she calling him *Thomas* instead of Tom all of a sudden? They'd spoken plenty of times before, and even had lunch once. It wasn't as if she might have forgotten it all of a sudden.

Unless…

The smirk formed unbidden on his lips. 'I'm sorry, *Violet*. I thought you were your sister for a moment. And it's Tom.'

'That's okay. You're not the only one to get confused.' She pulled a frustrated face, and Thomas couldn't help but laugh. It was just so *familiar*. And not from Rose.

'What?' Violet asked, obviously startled by his outburst. Maybe he should have had caffeinated coffee. Obviously the sleep deprivation was starting to affect him.

'I'm sorry,' he managed, trying to keep his smirk in check. 'But for a moment you looked just like you did in the—' Self-preservation kicked in as her face turned stony and he cut himself off.

'No, really. Do continue.' Her cut glass accent was sharp enough to wound, and any humour Tom had found in the situation ebbed away. 'I believe you were about to finish that sentence with the words "leaked sex tape", right?'

'I'm sorry,' Tom started, realising he'd apologised to this woman more in the first three minutes of meeting her than he'd normally need to in even a month of *dating* someone. But Violet interrupted before he could get to the part about sleep deprivation and inadequate impulse control.

'That's right,' she said, a little louder than Tom thought was strictly necessary. 'I'm the famous Huntingdon-Cross Sex Tape Twin. Not one of the two sisters who found true love and settled down. The one who men only want so they can film us together and put it on the Internet. Get your autographs here.'

The café was almost empty, but a couple of guys sitting at the table nearest the front definitely had their camera phones out. What kind of audacity did it take to stand up in public and admit to being the star of a ridiculously explicit sex tape watched by half the world? The sort only the rich and famous had.

'And apparently, according to the frustrated and annoyed look on my face, it can't even have been good sex. Personally, I don't remember, but Mr Buckley here has obviously watched it often enough to be considered an expert. Do feel free to ask him questions, if you like. I'm not in a hurry. I mean, I'm only missing my parents' marriage renewal ceremony to be here. Carry on.'

Waving an imperious hand towards him, Violet perched on the edge of a stool by the counter and waited. Feeling the heat of embarrassment in his cheeks, Tom grabbed the last of his things from the table and headed for the exit. Violet Huntingdon-Cross might be used to this sort of exposure, but he certainly wasn't.

'No questions? Oh, what a shame. I suppose we'd better be on our way, then.' Violet hopped down and followed him out into the arrivals hall.

'I suppose I deserved that,' he muttered as she held the door of the terminal open for him. He had laughed first. But she'd been over an hour and a half late to collect him. So the sleep deprivation was at least partly her fault, right?

'I suppose you did,' she replied. 'And I'm very sorry for being late to collect you. Rose gave me the wrong flight times.'

Damn. There went that argument.

'This is where you apologise to me for humiliating me in front of a crowd of people,' Violet prompted, and Tom raised his eyebrows.

'Me? Trust me, sweetheart, you did the humiliating all by yourself.' As if a performance of that sort was second nature to her. Which, judging by the sex tape, it might well be. He'd heard that Violet had calmed down in more recent years, but maybe the family had just got better at hiding her exploits from the media.

Her whole face flushed bright red at his words, and she pushed past him as they left the terminal. 'I'm parked in the short stay car park,' she called back over his shoulder.

He was pretty sure he wasn't supposed to hear her muttered words as she strode off towards the car, but he did. 'Hopefully not as short as your stay with us, though.'

Tom allowed himself a smile. Violet Huntingdon-Cross was definitely a worthy interview subject. And if he could get some new or hidden scandals on the eldest family wild child to help sell his book proposal, well, he'd be an idiot not to. Right?

CHAPTER THREE

VIOLET'S HANDS WERE still shaking as she tried to get the key into the ignition. At the back of the car, Tom was struggling to open the boot for his cases, but she had no intention of helping. Not least because the way her body was trembling meant she'd probably be even worse at it than him.

What on earth had possessed her? Eight years of best behaviour, of keeping her head down, of politely ignoring all the comments and jokes—all gone in one moment of frustration and humiliation in an airport coffee shop.

It had been his laugh, she decided, as the key finally slid home. It had made it so abundantly clear that she wasn't a real person to him, just a hilarious anecdote. One she had probably now ensured he would be dining out on for all time.

She was used to being seen as a public figure more than herself. She was always Rick and Sherry's daughter first, and often Rose or Daisy's sister before she was ever a person in her own right. Except when she was the Sex Tape Twin. And, quite honestly, she'd rather be nobody than *that*.

Except that was all she ever seemed to be to anyone outside her own family. And God, was she sick of it.

The car boot slammed shut; Tom must have managed to stow his cases away. Any moment now he'd slide into

the passenger seat beside her and they'd have to make po-
lite conversation all the way home. That, or sit in frosty
silence. Violet wasn't sure which would be worse.

She sighed. Yes, she was. Silence would be worse. Because only her dad had any idea how long Thomas Buckley
would be staying at their house, and she couldn't simply
send him to Coventry indefinitely. This wasn't boarding
school; it was real life. And somehow that had turned out
to be even more confining and stifling than the strict Cath-
olic school they'd all been sent to.

She was a grown-up now. The mistakes of her youth
were *supposed* to be in the past. She was more than the
stories people told about her. Which meant sucking it up
and making nice with the offensive American music journalist who would be writing some sort of tell-all about her
family and their life any time now. And hoping he'd forget
what a disaster this whole night had been.

It was like her dad had said, back when That Tape had
first hit the internet and suddenly her sex face was splashed
all over magazines and newspapers everywhere. He'd left
the rest of the band in some hotel somewhere, mid-tour,
and come home to check on her. While she'd lain sobbing
on her bed, he'd rubbed her back and told her, 'At least you
know now, honey. Not everyone out there wants what's best
for you. And only you can decide who to trust.'

Well. There was an easy answer to that one, Violet had
found. Don't trust anyone—except family.

Will had been an exception to the rule, and a hard-won
one at that. But it helped that he'd only ever been friend
material. She wouldn't trust even her best friend with her
whole heart. Not like Rose had done.

The passenger door opened and Violet sucked in a
breath before plastering on a smile. 'All okay?'

Tom gave her a slightly wary look, as if uncertain

whether she might just drive off with him half in and half out of the car. She couldn't really blame him; she hadn't been exactly consistent since they'd met.

Time to start mending fences before he started writing articles.

'Fine.' Tom slid into the seat beside her. 'And, uh, you?'

She forced her smile to brighten further. 'Just dandy.'

'Right. And are you always prone to such extreme mood swings?'

Oh, God, he was probably thinking that she was on drugs, or bipolar, or something else that would make a good story. This was *not* going well.

Violet sighed. Time to try honesty. 'Okay, look. We got off to a rotten start here, I know. But Dad wants you staying with us, working with him, and Dad doesn't change his mind once it's made up. So I just have to suck it up and get on with things, right? And since I don't particularly want to spend the next however many weeks avoiding you or trading insults on sight, I figure the easiest thing is to pretend the last half an hour didn't happen. Okay?' Partial honesty, anyway. She didn't need to mention—

'Plus you don't want me to tell the story of this evening in any future articles or books?'

Damn. 'Well, do you blame me?'

Tom was quiet so long that she had to glance over to check that he hadn't fallen asleep. When she looked, he was holding out his hand.

Eyebrows raised, she took it, biting her lip at the slight tingle she felt at his skin against hers. For heaven's sake, it was a handshake! Had it really been so long since someone she wasn't related to by blood or marriage had touched her that her body had forgotten what it felt like?

'I'm Tom Buckley,' he said with a half smile. 'Nice to meet you. Thanks for coming to pick me up.'

'Violet Huntingdon-Cross. Sorry I was an hour and a half late.'

He chuckled. 'Let's just blame Rose for everything, yeah?'

'That's what I've been trying to do for the last twenty-seven years,' Violet said, and sighed. 'Sadly, it never seems to stick.'

At Tom's laugh, she slipped the car into gear and pulled out of the parking space. 'Come on. Let's get you home. I bet you're tired after your long journey.'

'Exhausted,' Tom admitted, and when she looked she could see the dark circles under his eyes, even in the poor lighting of the airport car park. 'That's kind of my excuse, actually. For, well, everything. Sleep deprivation. It's been a hell of a week.'

'I'm sure. Rose said you were working out in Miami?'

He nodded. 'For the last week. Then a flying visit home to New York to repack my bags, then straight here. I feel like I haven't slept in a month. I'm looking forward to some peace and quiet, actually. Your dad told me that Huntingdon Hall is out in the middle of nowhere, right?'

'Ye—es,' Violet said, biting her lip as she remembered the party she'd left just a couple of hours before. It was long gone midnight. Surely everyone would have gone home by the time they arrived, right? Oh, who was she kidding? Rick and Sherry's parties were legendary. They'd be lucky if they didn't find anyone passed out on the tennis court in the morning, this time.

'That sounds ominous,' Tom said. 'Do they have guests? Wait...' Glancing over, she saw him frown, the moment it clicked into place for him. 'Oh, hell. It's their vow renewal today, right? You said you were missing it... That's why you were so annoyed about having to come and fetch me?'

'And why I'm wearing this fetching yet inappropriate

dress,' Violet confirmed. No need for him to know that, actually, she'd been happy to get out of there. 'I'm afraid there's a very real chance the party might still be ongoing.' She glanced at the dashboard clock. 'In fact, I think Dad and the boys will probably be taking the stage for their encore session right about now.'

Tom groaned and let his head fall back against the head-rest. 'So, no sleep tonight is what you're telling me.'

'Basically. Sorry! Maybe you can get some sleep in the car?' She should feel worse about this. The guy was obviously exhausted to the point of losing all social niceties. She should feel bad that her parents and their friends were going to keep him up for *another* night.

She really, really didn't, though.

It seemed to Tom that no sooner had he closed his eyes than a car door was slamming, then another opening, and cool night air flooded over his face. Followed swiftly by his ears being assaulted by one of The Screaming Lemons' classic hits being played as an acoustic number.

Normally, he'd be up at the front of the stage, soaking in the moment, tucking the memories away for future articles, trying to find the right words to describe the perfection of that three and a half minutes.

Tonight—or rather this morning—he just wanted it all to go away. Including Violet Huntingdon-Cross.

'Wake up, Sleeping Beauty,' she said, in a voice far too jolly for someone who had recently glared at him with such loathing. 'You're missing the party.'

He cracked open one eyelid and waited for the yellow blur of her hair, the pale fuzz of her face and the purple blotch that was her dress to come into focus. Then he blinked; she was closer than he'd thought, and suddenly the only things in focus at all were her bright blue eyes, peering down at him.

'Oh, good,' she said, straightening up. 'I thought for a moment I was going to have to leave you here for the night. That or get someone to come carry you to bed. That sort of thing never makes a terribly good first impression, you know.'

Unlike, for instance, pointing out a woman's sex tape history within five minutes of meeting her. God, when he woke up properly he was going to have to work at getting Violet back onside. As the only daughter living at home, he had a feeling she could make life difficult for him if she wanted.

And he rather suspected she might more than want to. It might actually be her burning life ambition at this point.

'I'm awake,' he half lied, forcing himself to straighten up. Another couple of moments and he might even make it out of the car.

Violet grabbed his hand and, even through his sleep fog, he couldn't help but be aware of the feel of her smooth, cool skin, or the way something indefinable crept up his arm at her touch. Something that seemed to crackle with possibilities.

Something that woke him up completely.

Blinking again, he twisted round to get his feet firmly on the ground and stood up, belatedly aware that he was still gripping onto Violet's hand, probably rather tighter than she'd like.

He dropped it fast, but her blue, blue eyes were still fixed on his and the puzzled crease between her eyebrows told him that whatever he'd felt, she'd felt it too.

At least he had the excuse of sleep deprivation. What justification was she using?

Violet shook her head and stepped back, nicely out of

his personal space. 'I know you're exhausted. But given that sleep is likely to be impossible for the next couple of hours at least, and since you *are* here to observe and interview and write about the band... Why don't you come and meet Dad?'

Dad. Even after an hour in the company of one of the most famous celebrity kids in the world, it still felt strange to hear her refer to the infamous Rick Cross as 'Dad'. How different a world must Violet live in to the real one he inhabited, to so casually be able to think of Huntingdon Hall as home, and one of the most recognisable couples ever as Mum and Dad?

Different, certainly, to the kid from New York who never even knew who his father was, only that he wouldn't have done him any good in life if he'd stuck around anyway. The kid whose mother had so disapproved of the method he'd used to get out of the gutter, she hadn't spoken to him for three years before her death.

Yeah, there were worlds between him and Violet. And however long he stayed at Huntingdon Hall, he had to remember that.

'Isn't he still playing?' Tom said, hoping it wasn't painfully obvious he was stalling. Rick had seemed sharp on the phone, the sort to see through people's masks. He wanted to be on top form when he sat down with Rick for the first time.

Violet tilted her head to the left, listening to the music, he presumed. 'This is usually his last number. He'll be off stage soon and still on that performance high. It's a good time to meet him if you want him to like you.'

'And do *you* want him to like me?' Tom asked. It seemed strange that she would, given everything.

A look of annoyance flashed across Violet's face, as if

she weren't used to being asked this many questions about her motives and feelings. Maybe she wasn't. 'Yes.'

Tom couldn't resist. 'Why?'

'Does it matter?' Violet tossed her hair back over her shoulder as the last chord rang out from the stage. 'We're going to miss him.'

'You haven't answered my question.' Tom folded his arms, leant back against the car and waited.

With an impatient huff, Violet grabbed his hand and started dragging him towards the stage. Tom didn't budge until she started talking.

'Because Dad makes up his mind about people and things in an instant, and that's it. You're here; you're going to be writing about him and us. If he likes you, he'll show you his best side, the stuff *I* want you to be writing about. If he takes a dislike to you…'

'Things could get messy?' Tom guessed.

Violet sighed as they reached the edge of the stage area. Even though the party was obviously filled with friends and family, the cheering as the band came off stage was still as loud as Tom had heard in any stadium.

'Let's just say this whole experience will be a lot less fun. For all of us.'

Suddenly, the familiar craggy face of Rick Cross appeared at the top of the stage steps, mouth open and laughing at something his band mate was saying behind him.

'Showtime,' Tom whispered, and Violet flashed him a quick grin—the first honest smile he'd seen from her.

Tom took a breath. Time to meet the parents.

CHAPTER FOUR

VIOLET HID A grin at the slightly shell-shocked look on Tom's face as Dad and the boys traipsed down the temporary stairs at the side of the stage set, all laughing, chatting and still clearly caught up in their own world—a world that consisted of music, noise and melodies.

She knew the kind of impact they could have, just off stage. When she was younger, just old enough to be allowed to stay up to watch the occasional gig from the wings, she and Rose had found it hard to understand this part—when Dad wasn't Dad, just for a moment. He was all Rick Cross, rock star, right now. And that was a sight to behold.

The adrenaline would wear off soon enough, Violet knew. He'd come down, hug his wife, ask for a drink, and before too long he'd be heading to bed to sleep it off. Well, maybe after a little more time with his closest friends—drinking and talking and probably singing.

Right now, in this moment, he was exactly who Tom Buckley had come here to interview. She hadn't lied when she said that this was the best time for Tom to make a good impression with her father. But it was also the best time to remind Tom that this wasn't just *anybody* he'd come here to write about.

The press could publish all the stories they liked about

her and her sisters—and heaven knew they would. But they couldn't touch her parents. Rick and Sherry were rock royalty, beyond reproach. There were no affairs, no addictions, no mistakes made—nothing to latch on to and use to make their lives hell. It might have been different back in the day, but not any more.

Now they were national treasures, and Violet was unbearably proud of them for it.

'Mr Cross.' Stepping forward, Tom stuck out his hand, smiling warmly. Violet had to give him credit—if he hadn't been slumped over in her passenger seat for the last forty-five minutes, she'd never have known he was utterly exhausted. He looked professional, ready to do a great job.

She just hoped that Dad's idea of a good job and Tom's meshed.

'Mr Buckley, I presume!' Rick's famous smile spread across his face. 'Great to have you here.' He shook Tom's hand with what looked like painful enthusiasm. 'Boys, this is the guy I've invited over to write our musical life story.'

'And your family's,' Tom put in. Violet rolled her eyes. As if any of them would forget that he was here to expose all their private lives as well as their public personas.

'Oh, he's here for the dirt, Rick.' Jez—Uncle Jez to the girls—the band's lead guitarist and Rick's best man, elbowed his friend in the ribs. 'Time to hide those skeletons in better closets!'

Rick laughed, his head tipped back in pure amusement and joy. Violet bit the inside of her cheek and just prayed there wasn't anything hidden there that she didn't know about. She couldn't imagine how there could be, given how closely she'd been involved in her parents' lives and work since she'd moved back home eight years ago.

But you could never be too careful when it came to the

press. And if Dad had any secrets, Uncle Jez would be the one to know them.

'Trust me, I'm just here to write the best, most honest story I can for your legion of fans. They're only interested in the truth.' Unlike Tom, presumably.

'And that's just what you'll get.' Rick clapped a hand on Tom's back, and Violet knew the reporter had passed some test that no one but her father would ever understand. 'The complete unvarnished truth, ready to be written down for posterity.'

Relief warred with apprehension inside her, and Violet clenched her fists so tightly her nails bit into the palms of her hands. On the one hand, the fact that her dad liked Tom would make the interviews go more smoothly, reducing the chances of a story about a recalcitrant, difficult star. On the other, it opened up the opportunity that Rick would get *too* close to Tom. As much as he talked about the unvarnished truth, surely her father realised there were some parts of their family lives, and history, that none of them wanted shared with the world. For the umpteenth time in some cases.

Well, there was nothing for it now but to see how things went. And try and keep tabs on both Tom and Rick, so she could try and head off any prospective trouble *before* it turned up in the papers this time.

'Darlings, you were brilliant as always.' Sherry floated up to them, kissing each of the band members on the cheek before planting a rather more thorough kiss on her husband. Tom, Violet noticed, was politely staring at the floor. Everyone else was too used to it to even bother.

'Mum, this is Tom Buckley,' Violet said once the public display of affection was over. Might as well get all the introductions over in one go. 'He's the writer Dad—'

'The writer who's going to tell our little story! Of

course.' Sherry held out a hand, although whether she intended it to be kissed or shaken Violet wasn't sure.

Tom went for the handshake. Not fully charmed yet, then. Mum might have her work cut out with this one. Obviously he wasn't taken in by her disingenuous description of his subject matter. Nobody in the world would describe the history of The Screaming Lemons and the Huntingdon-Cross family a 'little story'. Least of all anyone who had lived it.

'It's a pleasure to meet you, Mrs Huntingdon-Cross,' Tom said, releasing her hand.

'Oh, call me Sherry, please.' Mum flashed that legendary wide smile, the one that had been seen in magazines and on billboards for decades now. 'Anyone who stays here at Huntingdon Hall rather automatically becomes part of the family, I'm afraid. You might as well get used to it!'

Tom Buckley, part of the family? Not on Violet's watch.

But that was the problem with her parents. It wasn't that they were overly trusting or naïve, particularly. They knew the dangers of fame as well as anyone, and took care to live their lives circumspectly. But once they'd taken someone in and claimed them as a friend…it took a lot to shake their faith in them. And that could be dangerous.

'Where's Daisy?' Violet asked. She needed backup here and, with Rose and Will already gone on their honeymoon, Daisy-Waisy was going to have to be it.

'Oh, she and Seb have already turned in, I think,' Sherry said with a dismissive wave of her hand. 'Daisy was exhausted, poor thing—pregnancy is extraordinarily tiring, you know,' she added as an aside to Tom, who nodded, despite the puzzled crease between his eyebrows. 'And I think Seb wants to get off back to Hawkesley first thing.'

Curses. With Tom about to collapse from sleep deprivation, the chances weren't good that he'd be up in time to meet Daisy before she left. Which meant Violet was on her own trying to keep this whole project from blowing up in their faces. Lovely.

'And Rose has already left?' Tom asked politely. 'I met her in New York last month, and I know she'd planned to be here right through until the concert...' He left the sentence open. Not actually a question, so not really prying, but enough that politeness insisted that someone fill the gap. Tricky.

'Oh, yes,' Sherry said, beaming. 'She and Will left on their honeymoon a couple of hours ago.'

Tom's eyebrows inched up towards his hairline, and Violet winced. 'Honeymoon?' he asked. 'I didn't realise that she was planning a wedding.'

Or that she was even dating anyone, just like the rest of them. In fact, Violet was willing to bet that what Tom really meant was: *Two daughters married in a suspiciously short space of time, and one of them pregnant...there has to be a story here.* Especially if he'd seen the photos of Will and Rose in the papers.

Time to put a stop to that.

'Oh, yes,' she said, smiling cheerily. 'Will has practically been a part of the family for years now. We're delighted that they've made it official.' All true—Will *was* part of the family—certainly more than Tom Buckley ever would be. And why did he need to know that up until the last month or so, Will had only been there as Violet's best friend? And if he never realised that Will and Rose hadn't met until Daisy's wedding...well, that would be great. She just hoped that Tom Buckley didn't keep up with the UK celebrity gossip too closely.

Rick slung an arm around Tom's shoulders as the rest of the band wandered off in search of a drink or a bed. He had to reach up quite a bit to do it, Violet realised.

'That's the only downside of having daughters, you know,' Rick said, grinning at Violet. 'Having to give them away to unworthy men.'

'Oh, hush,' Sherry said. 'You know you adore Will. And Seb is going to be a wonderful son-in-law.'

'True. I have lucked out.' Rick turned his wicked grin onto Violet, and she felt her stomach clench at what he might come out with next. The inability to keep his inappropriate comments to himself was definitely a downside to the post-performance adrenaline. 'Makes me worry who Violet might decide to bring home. I can't possibly get that lucky three times in a row.'

Heat flooded Violet's cheeks. She'd spent more time blushing in front of Tom Buckley than actually talking to him at this point, she was sure.

'*Not* something you need to be worrying about, Dad.' Or be talking about in front of reporters.

Rick's face turned a little sad. 'No, I suppose not.'

'Anyway, Rose will be back soon enough, and you'll be able to catch up with her then,' Violet said with forced jollity. Tom gave her a look that left her in no doubt he knew exactly what she was doing—steering the conversation away from anything interesting. Violet made a mental note to warn Rose that it might look better if her whirlwind romance with Will hadn't been quite so...whirlwind-like. Rose would understand. Once she got home, everything would be so much easier.

'Actually, darling,' Sherry said, her smile just a little too wide, 'I spoke to Will as they were leaving. I understand they're going to be away for four weeks.'

Four weeks. Suddenly, with Tom Buckley standing there, it seemed longer than ever. Just when she really needed her twin at home with her. What had Will been thinking? Not about his best friend, stuck at home with the man who wanted to ferret out all her secrets. No, he'd been thinking about getting her twin sister naked for longer.

Damn men and their inability to think about more than one thing at once.

'That's right,' she said, forcing a smile. 'Although I couldn't get him to say where they were going.'

'Me neither,' Rick said. 'Will said he couldn't risk it. You know your mum would have texted Rose on the way to the airport and ruined the surprise.'

'Anyway. They won't be back until two days before the Benefit Concert, but Will said he'd left Rose's notes with you.' Mum had her 'tiptoeing' voice on. As if she was taking the long way round getting to the point.

'Yeah, it's all in Rose's study, apparently. Her black planner and all the files and contracts and stuff.'

'And…Will mentioned that you'd agreed to, well, keep an eye on things while they were away.' Ah, that was what Mum was working up to. Of course. Concern that Violet had agreed to something that, when it came down to it, she wouldn't be able to, or want to do.

Well, maybe it was time for her to prove her parents— and Tom Buckley—wrong. If Rose could organise a benefit concert, so could she.

'That's right.' And she'd do it too. But she really didn't want to get into this with Tom standing right there. Then again, there wasn't a chance of her getting any sleep tonight if they didn't agree a plan for the concert. The last thing they needed was the annual benefit being an utter disaster zone because Rose wasn't there, the one year they had a reporter on site recording all the behind the scenes activity for posterity.

Damn it! How could Will and Rose do this? Clearly, love had driven them crazy. It was the only explanation.

'You're looking worried, honey.' Her dad wrapped an

arm around her waist and hauled her close for a hug. 'But there's nothing to fret about. Rose has been running this thing like clockwork for years. The set-up's all done; everything's been booked for months.'

Violet turned her head to raise her eyebrows at her father. If everything was already sorted, then why was Rose always running around like a mad thing in the last few weeks before the concert every other year?

'Maybe your dad is being a little optimistic,' Sherry said. 'But really, darling, everything is in hand. All that's left is the fiddly last-minute stuff. And I'm sure we can find someone to handle that, if you don't want to. Rose and Will would understand. I'll call up an agency or something.'

Agency staff. Another stranger in their home all the time, taking responsibility for the biggest concert in The Screaming Lemons' calendar. Someone who had absolutely no reason to care if things went perfectly or just well enough to get paid.

Violet risked a glance at Tom. She could almost read the story writing itself behind his tired eyes. Thoughtless wild child celebrity daughter disappears on eve of major charity event after whirlwind romance, leaving benefit concert in chaos. Sex Tape Twin decides she'd rather pick flowers than take on the job.

Almost as bad a start as her scene in the coffee shop.

'No. I can do it. We don't need to call the agency. I'll take care of the concert. I've seen Rose do it, and I'm sure she's left really good notes. I can do it. I'd like to.'

A complete lie. The last thing she wanted to do, when she should be keeping an eye on Tom, was take on a high profile project that would put her in the public eye and require speaking to all the people she'd been happily avoiding for eight years. But sometimes proving a point—especially to someone like Tom Buckley—required sacrifice.

'Are you sure, darling?' Her mother's perfect face crinkled up into a frown. 'It doesn't really seem like…well, like your sort of thing.'

Of course it didn't. As much as she might have moaned about her parents calling Rose in to organise their wedding, she knew exactly why they'd done it. To spare Violet the misery of having to brave the public and the publicity again. It was bad enough doing so as a guest at endless charity functions, or just appearing at the benefit concert. Anywhere there were cameras, her nerves started to tremble. And this…this would mean liaising with pop stars, working with celebrities.

There were going to be a *lot* of cameras. Her fingers felt shaky just thinking about it.

'I'm sure,' she said as firmly as she could. 'The Benefit Concert is important. I want to make sure everything goes just as well as it would if Rose was here.'

Maybe she could just pretend to be Rose. Maybe no one would notice that she was actually the *other* twin. You know the one.

'Well, honey, if you're sure.' Rick's forehead had matching creases. Then he broke into a smile and clapped Tom on the back. 'Hey, maybe Tom here can give you a hand!'

CHAPTER FIVE

TOM COULDN'T BE sure if it was the sleep deprivation or if he really was missing something in the conversation going on around him. It felt as if there were actually two discussions taking place—one with words and one entirely conducted through concerned eyebrow gestures.

Still, he was pretty sure he didn't stand a chance of understanding the eyebrow conversation until he got some actual sleep. In fact, he was just plotting the best way to get shown to his room when Rick volunteered him.

'Me?' Tom wished that had come out slightly less squeakily. 'Help with the Benefit Concert?'

Sherry clapped her hands together. 'What a brilliant idea! I knew I married you for a reason.' She planted another kiss on her husband.

Violet, Tom noticed, hadn't responded at all. In fact, she looked as though she'd been sent into a state of severe shock and might need therapy to even deal with the idea.

God, he just had the best way with women, didn't he?

'Unless…Violet, darling, are you sure you really want to do this?' Sherry's eyebrows were doing the very concerned thing again, mirrored by Rick's. Yeah, Tom was definitely missing something here.

But Violet shook off the shock, smiled widely and said, 'Of course I do! And I'd appreciate any help that Tom is able to give me, in between the work he's *actually* here to do.' She even managed a sincere smile for him as she spoke, which Tom thought might be a first.

'Well, that's settled then.' Rick clapped his hands together, but his eyebrows suggested that nothing was settled at all. Tom suspected there'd be some private family conversations going on once he'd finally found a bed to fall into.

Well, so be it. Despite Sherry's enthusiastic welcome, he wasn't actually family. He didn't need to know all their tiny moments and their every word. He just wanted the stories. And, he'd admit it, the secrets. *They* were what would set his book apart from everything else ever written about Rick Cross and co.

And he was pretty sure he'd get them. Starting tomorrow.

'Guys, if I'm going to be ready to start interviews, write a book *and* organise the best concert in the history of benefit concerts, I'd better get some sleep.' Tom gave them all his friendliest all-in-this-together smile.

'Oh, of course!' Sherry immediately went into hostess mode, something Tom imagined she had honed and perfected over years of events, guests and parties. 'Violet, why don't you show Tom to his room, darling?'

Violet's smile was starting to look a little fixed, but no one except Tom seemed to notice. 'Of course. I might turn in myself.' She kissed her parents on their cheeks. 'It was a brilliant day. Here's to many more happy years of marriage.'

Tom followed Violet away from the stage, across the gardens. The party had obviously started to wind down after the Lemons had left the stage. The fairy lights in the trees shone down on abandoned glasses and plates and grass-stained marquee floors. A few stragglers still loitered by the temporary bar, where the last remaining barmaid yawned expansively, but most people had already headed home to bed.

Tom applauded their sensible natures. Of course, it was gone 4:00 a.m., so maybe they weren't that sensible.

Glancing over his shoulder, Tom saw Rick and Sherry making their way across to where the rest of the band sat with their partners or friends under the moonlight. Jez was strumming an acoustic guitar and laughter and conversation floated among the notes in the night air.

'I don't know how they're still going,' Violet said, following his gaze. 'I'm knackered. But they're always the last ones standing at a party. I think it's a point of pride these days. And they always finish the night together, just the gang of them who've been there from the start.'

He should be over there, soaking up the moment. Taking in the atmosphere that would make his book authentic. Except…it was a private moment and he was new on the scene. He couldn't force his way into that close-knit group. He had to earn his place, and that would take time and trust.

Violet was giving him an odd considering look. 'You still want to go to bed?' A slight flush of colour hit her cheeks in the pale lights, and he knew somehow that she was waiting for him to make a joke about whether that was an offer to join him. So he didn't.

'Alone, I mean. Not with me,' Violet babbled, as if he had. She must get that a lot, although he'd expected her to just brush it off or turn it back on the joker to embarrass *them*. After her display in the airport café, he knew she had the confidence and the fire.

Except…here, now, this seemed like a different Violet. One who'd known humiliation and pain. One he hadn't expected to meet when he'd sat in Miami and New York reading up about the wild child Sex Tape Twin without shame.

She'd never even put out a statement, he remembered. No apology for being a bad role model, for letting down her fans or those young girls who looked up to her. No regret for the shame and embarrassment she'd brought on her family.

Why was that? Suddenly, he desperately wanted to know. But those questions too required patience and trust to be earned. Maybe in a few weeks. After all, they were going to be working on the concert together. He had all the time he needed to learn everything there was to know about Violet Huntingdon-Cross, and her family.

'Honestly, Violet, I think I'd pass out on you tonight even if it was an offer.' He gave her a friendly smile to show it was a joke, that he didn't mean any offence. But, as her gaze met his, even his exhausted body had a moment where it wished that wasn't the case. That maybe, just maybe, this beautiful, confusing woman might actually make that offer to him.

Which was clearly ridiculous. They had nothing in common. She'd never understand him or his life, and he'd long since grown out of sleeping with any beautiful woman who offered. He liked his sexual encounters to mean something these days. Maybe not true love and forever, but a meaningful connection at least.

He couldn't really imagine any connection between him and the self-absorbed daughter of a celebrity. Still, he felt a little relief as the colour in her cheeks faded and she gave a quick nod.

'Come on then. Your bedroom's this way.' Violet started off towards the main staircase.

Tom bit his tongue to stop himself asking where hers was as he followed.

Violet woke up exhausted. Maybe it was all the excitement and chaos of the day and weeks before, but even once the big vow renewal was over and Rose was safely off on honeymoon she couldn't relax enough to sleep—despite the fact it had been gone four by the time she'd made it to bed. Eventually, after an hour of fitful tossing and turning, she'd given up and turned on her bedside light to read for a while.

She'd woken up four hours later, with the light still on and her face smooshed against her book. Not the perfect start to the day.

Scrubbing a hand across her face to try and persuade her eyes to stay open, she glanced at the clock. Nine thirty a.m. Chances were, the rest of the household would be sleeping in until well after lunch, but there was a nervous energy running through Violet's veins that she knew from experience wouldn't let her go back to sleep.

A shower, her most comfortable jeans and a T-shirt in her favourite shade of lavender-blue made her feel a little more human. She scraped her hair back into a clip to dry naturally, slathered on what claimed to be a rejuvenating moisturiser and headed downstairs in search of coffee.

'Coffee will make all things better,' she murmured as she switched on the espresso machine. The lie was a soothing one, at least. How could one poor drink be expected to deal with all the worries that had piled on in the last twenty-four hours?

'Think it can even help your poor old dad?' Rick leant against the door frame from the hall, his weathered face looking a little grey under his summer tan. 'I think I'm getting too old for the partying lark, honey.'

'Never.' Violet grabbed another espresso cup from the shelf. 'You'll still be rocking with a walking stick when the rest of us have grown old and boring.'

Except she didn't even need to age to grow old and boring; she was already there, wasn't she? Her entire existence already fitted within the grounds of Huntingdon Hall. Or it had. Maybe the Benefit Concert would be her chance to spread her wings.

'Only if I have my girls there to help hold me up,' Rick said, settling himself into one of the chairs at the kitchen table. 'Wouldn't be any fun without you all.'

'Mum sleeping in?' Violet handed her dad his coffee, then sat down to blow across the surface of her own cup.

'She says she needs her beauty sleep.' Rick laughed. 'Course, we all know she's plenty beautiful without it.'

'I didn't expect anyone else to be up for hours,' Violet said.

'I've got a shift down at the centre this morning,' Rick said. 'No one else could cover, so...' He shrugged.

Violet gave him a sympathetic smile. While everyone knew that Rick and Sherry supported all sorts of charities publicly, very few people were aware of all the private time they put in. Her dad did a lot of work for Alzheimer's charities, as well as helping out at a local drug rehabilitation centre, while her mum put in time on a children's helpline, amongst other things. Would they share that side of themselves with Tom? Violet had no idea.

'I'll be back to give Tom his first interview this afternoon, though,' Rick said, suggesting that he might. Violet was glad; more people should know about all the good they did. 'And what are you up to today?'

Violet sipped her coffee. 'I was planning on raiding Rose's files to get an idea of what I've let myself in for with this Benefit Concert.'

Rick's face turned serious. 'Now, honey, you know you don't have to take that on. It's not too late to change your mind.'

'Don't think I can do it, huh?' Violet said, eyebrows raised.

'Violet, I truly believe you could do anything in the world you dreamt of, if you decided to. It just comes down to if you really *want* to.'

Violet bit her lip. Dad thought she could do it. He had faith in her. And maybe, just maybe, he knew something she didn't. At the very least, she wanted the *chance* to prove him right.

'I want to do it,' she said, ignoring the way her whole body felt as if it might start trembling any second. This was her chance—her golden opportunity to do that *something more* she'd been wishing for. 'It's important to me, and I think it's time.' Time to stop hiding behind the walls of Huntingdon Hall at last. Time to start living in the real world again, even if it was still filled with monsters.

The smile that split Rick's craggy face was reward enough for her decision. 'I think you might be right, honey,' he said, and pressed a kiss to her hand across the table. 'I think it's time the whole world got used to seeing the *real* Violet Huntingdon-Cross for once.'

Violet smiled back through her nerves. *Wouldn't that be something?*

CHAPTER SIX

HUNTINGDON HALL WAS ridiculously large, Tom decided, after getting lost on the way to the kitchen for the third time. Tastefully redecorated, with none of the attempts to recreate the Regency or whatever that he'd half expected from the almost aristocracy. But then, this family were unusual in almost every other way, why not this one too?

There were so many contradictions for him to uncover, but that was half the fun.

Contradiction one. Sherry had inherited this hall from her blue blood family—but had obviously renovated it entirely using her husband's money—or her own, Tom supposed. She had enjoyed a very lucrative modelling career, after all. Anyway, the point was, while the outside of Huntingdon Hall still looked like something from a period novel, the inside was entirely modern.

As Tom made his way down a corridor that looked almost exactly like the one he'd just explored, Violet's directions from the night before seemed even more ridiculous. *Just follow the walls,* she'd said. *Eventually all of them lead back to the main staircase.* Follow the walls? What kind of advice was that? Especially since it appeared he'd been following the walls in the wrong direction for the last five minutes. Why wasn't there a helpful servant around here somewhere?

Of course that led him to contradiction two. In a house this size, with a family this rich, he'd have expected dozens of flunkies running around doing things for them. But he'd seen nobody. Oh, he was sure there was a housekeeper somewhere, and he highly doubted that Sherry did her own cleaning, but apart from that? Everything seemed to be kept in the family. Rose took care of the band's PR and everything else that needed organising, it seemed.

At least until she ran away on her honeymoon and Violet stepped in, rather than hire someone else.

Violet was, without a doubt, most definitely contradiction number three.

Tom turned another corner, dutifully following the wall and, finally, stumbled across the staircase. At last, his path towards coffee and maybe even breakfast was clear.

He hopped down the stairs in double time, smiling as he heard voices coming from what he hoped would prove to be the kitchen. Part of him was surprised not to be the first up—it had been a ridiculously late night, but even with his exhaustion level he'd found it impossible to sleep past ten. Too many years of risking missing the tour bus or a flight somewhere had left him a very light sleeper.

'Good morning.' Both Rick and Violet looked up at his words, and Tom got the unerring feeling that he'd interrupted something.

'Ah! Our guest awakes.' Rick moved towards the coffee pot. 'Strong and black? Or do you drink what can only be described as "warm milk with a coffee scent" like my daughter?'

'Strong and black, please,' Tom replied. Actually, he normally preferred it somewhere in between, but he wasn't taking the chance of failing the Rick Cross coffee test. Or any other tests he threw his way before Rick actually opened up to him and gave him the material he needed.

Rick nodded as he poured. 'Good choice. Now, about today.' He handed Tom a tiny steaming espresso cup with an apologetic smile that made Tom's heart sink. There were going to be no interviews today, he just knew it.

This was always the risk in coming here. Staying at Huntingdon Hall gave Tom unprecedented access, yes. But it also gave the subject the illusion of limitless time—and plenty of excuses to dodge sitting down and talking to him.

Tom did not have limitless time, and he needed this story.

'I was hoping we could make a start on some questions about what the Lemons are doing now,' Tom said, hoping the allure of potential publicity for the new album would draw him in. 'I've got a couple of possible slots in maga-zines and supplements coming up, and it would be good to let people know what's next for the band.'

'Rose would kick me if she heard me turning down the publicity, but I'm afraid I have some commitments today that I need to take care of before I can sit down with you.' Rick reached for his own coffee mug—which, Tom no-ticed, had milk in it, damn him. 'Sorry, Tom. I'll be back this afternoon, though. And I'll get Sherry to book some time with you too, as well as the boys from the band. I want us to get the bulk of the first few interviews down over the next week or two, so we've all got more time to focus on the Benefit Concert when it comes around. That sound okay to you?'

'That's…great, actually.' So much for the old man try-ing to avoid the interviews. Maybe Rick Cross was as se-rious about this book as Tom hoped after all. 'And I can probably find something to entertain me around here this morning.'

He hadn't meant to look at Violet, but somehow his gaze just sort of slid over in her direction. Her blonde hair looked darker—was it wet?—and strands were curling around her face. In jeans and a bright blue T-shirt, without make-up, she looked a lot younger than she had the night before. And, from the redness around her eyes, more vulnerable.

What had she been discussing with her father before he walked in? Suddenly, Tom wished he'd stopped outside to eavesdrop.

'You can help Violet go through all Rose's files!' Rick sounded immensely pleased with himself at the idea. 'Get up to speed on all the plans for the Benefit Concert. I just know my Violet is going to knock this one out of the park.'

He reached across and squeezed his daughter's shoulder, and she gave him a rather weak smile in return.

'Still, everyone needs a little help sometimes, right, honey?' Rick went on.

'Yeah, I guess.' With a deep breath, Violet straightened her shoulders visibly and looked him in the eye. 'So, Mr Buckley, how about it? You up for a challenge?'

'Absolutely.' Tom drained his espresso and smiled, unsure if the challenge was the concert or understanding the woman sitting in front of him.

'Okay. So…Will said that Rose left everything she had to do with the Benefit Concert in here.' Violet approached the door to the seldom used study on the first floor with more than a little trepidation. She hadn't been in this room since it was their homework room, years ago. Since she'd handed in her dissertation, she hadn't so much as opened the door.

It was Rose's room, not hers. As close as the twins were, Violet had to admit that they'd lived very separate lives over the last few years. With Rose in New York, that distance had only grown.

Oh, they still talked about pretty much everything. Violet still knew her sister's mind and heart, and she knew that if she needed anything Rose would be there in a heartbeat. But their lives were different. Rose jetted around the world, building her career working for The Screaming Lemons' PR, but also cultivating her passion making jewellery. The wedding rings she'd crafted for Seb and Daisy, and the bracelet she'd designed and made for their mother, were amongst the most beautiful things Violet had ever seen. Rose had real talent, and Violet knew that Will would encourage that—especially now Rose had made the decision to give up the PR side of things and follow her dreams.

Maybe it was time for Violet to do that too, she thought as she pushed open the door. Starting with the Benefit Concert.

'Huh.' Behind her, Tom stared over her shoulder. 'Did Will say where, exactly?'

It was a valid question. Violet's heart sank as she took in the piles of paperwork, the overflowing files and the stack of wedding magazines on the desk. Poor Rose had been swamped for the last month or more, with preparations for the band's latest tour, album promotion and not to mention planning their parents' vow renewal service and party. No wonder she hadn't had time to tidy up.

Well, that just made step one in the 'get-back-out-there-and-show-the-world-what-Violet-Huntingdon-Cross-is-really-made-of' plan all the more obvious.

'We need to start with a clean sweep,' she said, picking up Rose's battered, precious black planner from the middle of the piles covering the desk. 'We'll sort through everything in here, clear up and find all the relevant stuff, then set up my office in here. Will sent me the link to the Dropbox folder Rose was using for all the electronic stuff, and she's given me access to the email account she uses for the Benefit Concert each year. So I should have every-thing I need to get started...'

'Once you can find the desk,' Tom finished for her.

'Yeah.' She turned to look at him. 'Sorry. This probably isn't what you were hoping to do this morning.'

Tom shrugged. 'Not entirely. But this afternoon should make up for it. And it doesn't have to be a total waste. I can ask you some basic interview questions while we're work-ing.' He pulled out his smartphone and scrolled through to an app with a microphone logo. 'You don't mind being taped, right?'

Violet's body froze, her back so stiff she thought it might snap. At least he was asking, she supposed. She hadn't been given that courtesy last time.

'I think maybe today we should just focus on getting this office sorted.' She knew her voice was stilted, but she couldn't seem to do anything about it. 'If I'm going to be on the record, I want to be sure I'm giving your questions my full attention.' That way, it would be harder for him to sneak in trick questions, or twist her words around later. She'd spent some time, after everything, researching the best way to deal with the media. Of course, when every question was about a sex tape, there was only so much you could do. But she knew more now than she had at nineteen and that knowledge gave her a little confidence, at least.

She could deal with Tom Buckley. As long as she kept her wits sharp.

'Okay. Fair enough.' Tom slipped the phone back into his pocket and Violet's shoulders dropped back to their usual level. If he had any idea why his request had her so rattled—and surely he must—Tom didn't show it. He was a professional, she supposed. 'So, where do we start?'

Violet surveyed the room. 'The desk? I mean, that's probably going to have her most recent stuff on it. And once we've cleared that, at least we have somewhere to work.'

'Sounds like a plan.' Shifting a pile of papers and a red polka dot cardigan from the leather chair on the visitor's side of the desk, Tom grabbed the first stack of files from the edge of the desk and took a seat.

Selecting her own pile, Violet settled into the desk chair and started to read.

'So, is your sister always this messy when she works?' Tom asked, and Violet's hackles instantly rose.

'She's been incredibly busy recently,' Violet said. 'I'm sure that, if she were here, she'd know exactly where everything was, though. She's very efficient.'

'I'm sure she is.' Tom dropped his first file onto the floor. 'That's my "wedding vow renewal" pile, by the way. I guess that must have taken up a lot of her time. You all helped, though?'

'Where we could,' Violet replied. Of course, with Daisy suffering from first trimester woes, and herself relegated to flower arranging, it had mostly been Rose. As usual. 'Mum was pretty burnt out from organising Daisy and Seb's wedding, so she left a lot of it to Rose. I took care of the flowers, though.'

Tom's gaze flicked up to meet hers, faint disbelief marring his expression. 'You arrange flowers?'

'I do.' Violet looked back down at the file in her hands. This, at least, had to be a safe topic. No one expected the Sex Tape Twin to spend her weekends fiddling with oasis and floristry wire in the church hall, right? 'I took over the local church flower committee a few years ago now.'

That, of course, had been a local scandal in its own way—she was too young, too inexperienced, or just had too much of a reputation. But, whatever anyone said, that scandal hadn't made the national press, at least.

'Huh. I always imagined church flower ladies were…'
Tom trailed off and Violet raised her eyebrows at him as
she waited for him to finish the sentence. 'Married?' he
said finally, as if asking her to tell him what to say to get
out of the conversation.

Violet huffed a laugh and reached for the next file.
'Married. That's the best you could do?'

'Well, okay, fine. I thought they were older, more boring, greyer and considerably less beautiful than you.'

Despite the warmth filling her cheeks, Violet resisted
the urge to say, *You think I'm beautiful?*

He'd just think she was fishing for compliments, anyway.

'As it happens, I'll have you know that floristry is more
popular than ever.' She had no idea if that were actually
true, but it sounded good. 'Young women across the country are taking courses in flower arranging.' Probably.

'Did you?' Tom asked. 'Take a course, I mean?'

'Not…exactly.' Damn. There went the legitimacy of
her words.

'So how on earth did you get to be head of the church
flower committee? I've watched enough rural British murder mysteries to know that kind of job is usually enough
to kill over.'

'We live in Buckinghamshire, not Midsomer,' Violet
pointed out. 'We haven't had a murder in the village in
almost seventy years.'

'Still, I bet there was a queue of blue-haired ladies waiting to take over. Weren't they a tad annoyed when you
swanned in and stole it from right under their noses?'

Well, yes, of course they had been. But Tom made it
sound as if she'd just rocked up and demanded she be given
the job because of who her parents were, just like some

people she'd known back in the day had demanded access to exclusive nightclubs. And usually been let in, too.

'I'd been trained up by the last head of the committee for five years,' Violet said, trying not to notice the lump that still formed in her throat when she thought about Kathleen. 'When she got sick, she insisted that I take over. She dictated arrangements to me over the phone, made me bring her photos to show her I was doing it right. When she died…I was voted in the day after the funeral.' Kathleen had actually tried to leave her the position in her will, but of course it hadn't been hers to give. So there had to be a ballot of the whole committee—which she'd won by just one vote.

Still, Violet hoped she'd won over the doubters over the last few years. God knew, she'd achieved very little else. Until now. It might be a bit of a jump from flower arranging to concert arranging but, come hell or high water, she'd prove herself here just like she had on the committee.

'But you obviously wanted it.' Tom tilted his head to one side as he studied her. It made Violet want to flinch, so she worked really hard at keeping her muscles still instead. He *wanted* her to flinch, she was sure of it. And she wasn't giving Tom Buckley *anything* he wanted.

'It meant a lot to Kathleen that I take it on,' she said evenly. 'And I get a lot of pleasure from working with flowers.'

He nodded absently, as if taking everything she said as accepted truth. But then he fixed her with his clear green eyes and said, 'So, tell me. How did the daughter of rock royalty go from starring in her very own porno to arranging the Easter flowers?'

CHAPTER SEVEN

Violet went very still for a moment, the fingers clutching her file almost white from tension. Tom sat back and waited. He knew this part. In any usual interview, this was the bit where the subject tried to recall all the advice from the PR guru on how to spin their misdeeds in the best possible light.

And Miss Violet Huntingdon-Cross had clearly had some ambitious PR advice, probably from her twin sister, actually. Keep your head down, take on some charity work, or work in the community. Rehabilitate your character until everyone forgets the part about how they saw you naked on the internet, mid pretty boring sex.

Was this why Rick had pushed for him to help her out with the Benefit Concert? Tom had no doubt that Rick's first concern was publicity for the band, but maybe the re-launch of his eldest daughter as an upstanding member of society was a nice side benefit. Hell, maybe that was why he was doing all this now. With two daughters married, he could happily portray them as settled down and mature—and Violet could ride in on their coat-tails.

Except Tom had seen her lose it in the middle of an airport café. He'd glimpsed the real passionate, wild Violet—and he really wasn't buying the Sunday school teacher act.

'I thought we agreed that this wasn't the time for an interview,' Violet said, her voice stiff and prim.

Tom shrugged. 'It's not. I'm not recording anything. Just asking an idle question.'

'Sure.' Violet's mouth twisted up into a bitter smile. 'I bet we're off the record and everything, right? No, thanks. I know how that works.'

'If I say something is off the record, I mean it.' Tom sat up straighter, bristling a little at the implication. 'Your dad brought me here because he knows my reputation as a fair, honest, accurate reporter. I'm not trying to trick you into anything here, Violet.'

He'd worked too hard at building up that reputation—after the story that made his name—to risk it now, over one blonde wild child. If his mother were still alive, even she'd have to admit that he'd turned it around. He was respectable now, dammit.

Violet met his gaze, her blue eyes wide and vulnerable. She'd probably practised that look in the mirror, too. 'Okay, then,' she said finally, giving him a small nod.

But she didn't answer his question. Instead, she turned back to the file in her hand, giving it her full attention as a little crease started to form between her eyebrows. Tom wanted to ask her what she was reading—until he realised there was a much more pressing question to be answered.

'What did you mean, when you said you "know how that works"?'

Violet shrugged, not looking up. 'You know. Off the record is only valid until someone says something worth breaking the rules for.'

'That's not true.' The defence of his profession was automatic—even as he admitted to himself that for some reporters it was entirely true. The sort of reporter who would hack voicemails or intercept emails didn't care very much about a verbal agreement about 'the record'. Hell, it was barely more than a social convention anyway, a nicety to make interview subjects feel more comfortable.

But he'd stuck by that convention for his entire career, bar one story. And he didn't intend to ever break it again.

'Really?' Violet raised her pale brows at him in disbelief. 'You really believe that all reporters honour the privacy of things said off the record?' She shook her head without waiting for an answer. 'The only way to be safe is to assume that you're on the record at all times. Whatever anyone says.' The way she said it, the conviction she gave the words…this wasn't just some advice from a media expert. This was the mantra Violet lived her life by—or at least it was now.

'When talking to reporters?' Tom asked, wanting her to admit to what he suspected. 'Or when talking to anybody?'

Her gaze slipped away from his. 'Depends on who you're talking to. And whether you trust them not to sell your story to the papers.'

'And who do you trust that much?' Tom had an inkling it would be a very short list.

'Who do you?' Violet threw his own question back at him, and he blinked in surprise.

'Trust me, no one is interested in any story about me.' Just the idea of it made him laugh. He was a reporter, always behind the scenes, shedding light on other people's lives. No one ever needed to examine his—and he really didn't want them to.

'Just suppose they were. Hypothetically.' Violet leant forward and, even with the desk between them, her piercing stare made her feel uncomfortably close. 'Imagine that something happened in your life—you won the lottery, or wrote the next Harry Potter, or married a celebrity, whatever. Suddenly everyone in the world wants to know your secrets. Who would you still tell the truth to?'

No one. The thought felt empty and hollow even as it echoed through his brain. There was no one he trusted with that much of him. No one he'd tell about his hopes and dreams—and no one he'd trust with his failures or regrets.

Oh, he had friends, plenty of them. Enough in every country that he always had someone he could meet for dinner, or go out for drinks with. And he'd had girlfriends, too—also plenty. The fact he didn't have one right now made absolutely no difference to the trusted person question. He hadn't told any of the previous ones any more than he thought they needed to know. His mother had probably been the last person he'd trusted that way, and she was a long time gone. Not to mention the fact that even telling *her* the truth hadn't ended so well.

He wasn't the story. He never was. That was kind of the point of being a reporter.

'Never happen,' he said as breezily as he could. 'My utter unremarkableness is one of the main reasons I've managed to build up a successful career as a music journalist. So, go on, your turn. Who do you trust that much? Rose, I imagine. And Daisy and your parents. Who else?'

'I think that's plenty, don't you?' Violet sat back and picked up her file again. 'After all, it's obviously still four more people than you have,' she added, not looking up.

Tom didn't have an answer to that one, either.

It was going to take them forever to wade through all of Rose's files. Violet bit back a sigh—Tom would only have a sigh-related question waiting for her. Maybe ask her if she was frustrated by her sister's departure or, worse, in love with her new brother-in-law. She had a feeling it was only a matter of time before someone noticed that Rose had married the man who'd been squiring her twin around for the last few years and jumped to the obvious—but erroneous—conclusion that there was a really juicy story there. She'd place money on it being Tom, and before the week was out.

Sneaking a glance at him across the desk, Violet considered the way he'd evaded his own question about who to trust in this world. On the one hand, she'd been surprised to find someone whose list was shorter than her own. But then, given his profession, perhaps that wasn't so surprising. He had to know that everyone had their price, when the story—or tape—was good enough.

Still, she'd have expected him to have *someone.* A trusty sidekick best friend, perhaps. Or a loyal, long-suffering girlfriend. Not everyone was lucky enough to have a built-in best friend from the day they were born, like she and Rose had been, but she'd have thought he'd have found at least one person to trust over the last few decades.

Strangest of all was the feeling she'd got, watching him dodge the question. The odd sensation that in that moment they'd both looked past a mask neither of them usually lifted, and seen something they never intended the other to see. Had he really seen her fear, her mistrust in a way that even her family couldn't quite grasp? Or had she imagined that strangely searching look?

And what about him? Had she truly recognised another person who understood that the truth was a private thing, that who a person was deep down didn't always need to be shared? At the least she knew he didn't trust people any more than she did.

Was he lonely? Or did he like being alone? Did it make it easier for him to do his job, not worrying about friends or family who might be disappointed in him, or disapprove of the stories he chose to tell?

Or had he had someone once and betrayed them for a story, like Nick had done to her?

Shaking her head, Violet looked back down at the file in her hand. She was projecting now. Whatever Tom's history was, and whomever he chose not to share it with, she was pretty sure it had nothing in common with hers.

Violet added the file in her hand to the 'album promo' pile and was just reaching for the next one when her phone buzzed in her back pocket. Standing to fish it out, she checked the name on the screen.

'It's Rose,' she said, her finger hovering over 'answer'. 'I'll go take it in the other room.'

'See if you can find out where she's hidden all the bands' contracts while you're at it,' Tom said. 'And the notes on the riders. They'd be really useful around now.'

Violet nodded and escaped into the sitting room next door to talk to her sister. She really didn't want an unreliable audience when she was talking to one of her four people.

'Hey, where are you?' Violet shut the door carefully behind her, just in case Tom got it into his head to eavesdrop. 'Is it glorious and sunny and beautiful?'

'All of the above,' Rose said with a laugh. 'I have to admit, Will has outdone himself. But you'll have to wait and see the photos when we get back. I want to see who guesses where we've been first.'

'Meanie.' Violet pouted but, since her sister couldn't see her, the effect was rather wasted. 'Are you happy, though?'

'Very,' Rose promised, her tone suddenly serious. 'Really, Vi…I'm so much happier than I thought I could be. Ever.'

Violet's heart ached at the truth in her sister's words. 'I'm so, so happy for you,' she said as sincerely as she could. But even as she spoke, she rubbed the space between her breasts, just over her heart, and wished that she could find such happiness.

'What about you?' Rose asked. 'How are things there?'

That, Violet knew, was her cue to tell her sister light-hearted stories about everything that had happened in the less than twenty-four hours since she'd left. Only problem was, she was struggling to think of any.

'Um, fine. Nothing much to report, really. Mum and Dad stayed up super-late with the guys, and Dad headed off for his shift at the centre today looking half dead, even after a couple of coffees. Mum still hadn't surfaced last time I checked.'

'So, the usual,' Rose summarised.

'Pretty much, yeah.'

'How about Tom? Did you find him okay at the airport?'

'Yeah, eventually.' Violet bit the inside of her cheek. She really, really wanted to point out that Rose had given her the wrong flight times. But if she did she'd have to explain what happened next. She was just trying to think of a way to fudge the subject when Rose spoke again.

'Hel—lo. What happened? Tell me immediately.'

'I don't know what you're talking about,' Violet lied.

'Yes, you do. That was your "I'm mad at you but don't know how to tell you" voice. Twin here, remember?'

'Okay, fine. You gave me the wrong flight times! He ended up calling and demanding to know where I was, so I rushed all the way over to Heathrow in my bridesmaid's dress and heels then humiliated myself in front of everyone in the coffee shop.' Violet finally took a breath and relaxed once the words were out. Not telling Rose stuff took far more energy than just telling her everything.

'Will just forwarded you his email with the flights on,' Rose said mildly. 'If they were wrong, it was his own stu-pid fault. Now, humiliated yourself how, exactly?'

Maybe it would have been worth holding back that part, though.

'His fault? Fantastic. So it was all over nothing in the end, anyway.' Violet sighed. 'I was so determined to make a good impression—to make him like us so he'd write nice things about us. But after his call and the traffic, I was kind of flustered. And it had been a really, really long day.' A long, loved-up, excruciating sort of day for the one single girl in a family of people madly in love with their spouses.

'Oh, God, what did you do?' Rose asked with the sort of dismayed expectation that came from having been witness to every single one of Violet's screw-ups for the past twenty-seven years.

'He thought I was you!' Violet said. Rose knew how much she hated that. And after the day she'd had…well, some sort of blow-up was inevitable.

'Tell me you didn't berate that poor man in public for not being able to tell apart identical twins he's barely met.'

'Of course not! In fact, I played along for a moment or two, but he figured it out pretty quickly.' Violet swallowed at the memory. She hated this bit, but Rose was going to hate it even more. 'He said he recognised my facial expression. From the video.' No need to say which one.

Silence on the other end. But only while Rose caught her breath, Violet imagined.

'I will fly home right now and beat him up if you want.' Rose swore, quite impressively. Violet recognised a few words they hadn't learnt at boarding school. 'I can't believe I thought he seemed like a good guy! I thought we could trust him with this interview, with Dad. But now… I'll call Dad. Get him to send him back to whichever rock he crawled out from under.'

Warmth filled Violet's chest at her sister's unqualified

support. But part of her couldn't help but feel a little responsible too.

'In fairness, he was severely sleep deprived and over-caffeinated at the time,' she said. 'And he didn't really say it in an offensive manner. Well, as far as you can remind someone of the biggest mistake of their life without meaning to offend them.'

'It wasn't your fault,' Rose said automatically, just as she had every time it had been mentioned for the last eight years. 'You trusted him. And you had no idea he was filming you—let alone that he'd put it out on the internet. Do not blame yourself for the actions of Nefarious Nick.'

'*Anyway,* I don't think Tom meant to cause offence. And I might have overreacted a little bit.'

'Overreacted?' Violet was pretty sure she could *hear* Rose wincing. 'What did you do?'

'Announced to the whole coffee shop that yes, I was the Huntingdon-Cross Sex Tape Twin and if they had any questions they should ask Tom, since he'd clearly watched it plenty of times.'

Rose let out a burst of laughter. '*Really?* Oh, that's brilliant. And the first time I've ever heard you joke about the whole thing.'

'I wasn't joking,' Violet muttered.

'So, did he make it to Huntingdon Hall alive? How are things going? I mean, after that kind of a start I'm assuming he's probably part of the family already.' Apparently, Rose's romantic happiness hadn't dulled her ability for sarcasm.

'Actually, we agreed to start over. He's helping me with the Benefit Concert.'

'You took it on?' Rose asked. 'I kind of hoped you might when Will said you'd agreed to take care of things. But I wasn't sure if you'd…well, feel comfortable doing it. You know, you can always get someone in from the agency we use if you're not happy.'

'It's fine. I said I'd do it and I will.' And hearing how everyone else expected her to pull out every five minutes was only making her more determined that it would be a raging success. 'Although we're having some fun trying to sort through all your papers.'

'Yeah, sorry about the mess. But there's a system, I promise.'

'Care to explain it to me?' Violet asked, settling back on the sofa to take detailed notes as Rose explained the meanings of different file colours, and how the left side of the desk was only ever used for pending stuff. She just hoped she and Tom hadn't already messed up whatever weird system Rose had developed…

CHAPTER EIGHT

TOM STARED AT the blank laptop screen in front of him, then rubbed his eyes. He'd been at Huntingdon Hall for almost a week, sat down for detailed, open interviews with both Rick and Sherry, plus most of the band members. He had hours of audiotape, plus a whole notebook full of scrawled notes. He'd even managed to put together a preliminary article for one of his favourite editors, talking about the exciting opportunity he had, staying at Huntingdon Hall. When it went to print in one of the supplements this weekend, it should build excitement for the Benefit Concert, help with the album promo and even start some buzz for the eventual band biography. It had been a productive, worthwhile week.

So why the hell was he still thinking about Violet Huntingdon-Cross, drowning in paperwork in her sister's study?

She was the only one he wasn't certain he could get to open up, that was all. He had appointments to talk with Daisy, and even her new husband, in a couple of weeks when they came for the benefit, and he felt sure he could collar Rose and the new Mr when they got back from their honeymoon. But Violet…she was right there in the house with him, and yet he couldn't get close. Even when they were in the same room, she made it very clear there was an exclusion zone around her—one he would never enter.

Maybe he'd got too close with their conversation about trust—even if he had come out the worst for it. But that only meant he needed to push a little further.

Tom closed his laptop. He could take a break from writing if it meant getting Violet to open up. After all, her parents were off doing the first of many promos for the Benefit Concert—radio today—her sisters were both busy being married and happy...it was just the two of them there now. They might as well get used to each other's company.

Another thing he had managed over the last week was learning his way around Huntingdon Hall. At least he no longer got lost looking for the kitchen.

Tom knocked on the study door, waiting for Violet to call for him to come in, but she didn't answer.

After a moment, Tom pushed the door open, just enough to peer through the crack.

'Yes, I understand that, Mr Collins. But—' Violet sat at the desk, phone clamped to her ear. Strands of hair were escaping from the clip she'd used to keep it back, and she rubbed her forehead with her free hand. 'And, as I've already told you—' A sigh, as she was presumably cut off again.

Slipping through the open door, Tom took the seat opposite the desk and she glanced up at the movement.

'Who is it?' he whispered.

'Olivia's manager,' she mouthed back. Damn it. Olivia was the hot new American act Rose had booked for the benefit. Tom had interviewed her once or twice before, and each time the star's list of demands had grown. Word in the industry was that no one could wait until her star burned out and she had to start begging *them* for the press. But while the kids were still downloading her music...

Reaching over, Tom stabbed the speakerphone button with his finger, and Mr Collins's diatribe became audible.

'All I'm saying is that I think I need to talk with someone with a little more authority over there. Olivia isn't just some local act, taking part for the exposure. She's the biggest thing in pop music right now, and I don't think that some girl who's only famous for who her parents are and for getting naked on the internet can really appreciate—'

'Mr Collins—' Tom struggled to keep his tone professional as inside him indignation and anger burned brighter '—this is Tom Buckley. We've spoken before, when I've been commissioned to write pieces about Olivia.'

'Tom. Right.' A little unease threaded through Mr Collins's words now he knew he was talking to the press. Tom didn't imagine for a moment that he had *much* power in the world, but the ability to make famous people look ungrateful, stupid or plain mean was always worth something. 'You're covering this concert?'

'I'm helping Miss Huntingdon-Cross organise it this year.' Maybe his words were a little sharp, but Mr Collins deserved a hell of a lot worse. 'All for charity, you know. I've got Olivia's rider right here.' He held out a hand and Violet passed it over. Tom scanned through the pop star's list of demands for her performance and backstage requirements, eyebrows raised. 'She does realise that all the profits from the day go to very worthwhile charities, yes?'

'Well, of course she does,' Mr Collins blustered. 'She's always keen to help those less fortunate than herself.'

'In which case, I'd imagine that she wouldn't want the sixty-seven requests she's made to result in us not being able to meet our giving targets for the year, right? I mean, I'm sure that nobody would ever say that Olivia places more importance on having the appropriately named Diva vodka available backstage than she does on starving children getting a hot meal, but…well, you have to admit, it doesn't look all that good.'

There was a pause on the other end of the line. Tom waited it out. The next move had to be the manager's.

'I'm sure Olivia would be satisfied with a more...easily available vodka,' Mr Collins said eventually.

Tom drew a gleeful line through the words reading 'Three bottles of Diva vodka' on the piece of paper in front of him. 'I'm sure she would too. In fact, why don't you go back to her and see which other items she might be willing to forgo? For the sake of the children.' And her publicity, of course. Tom was under no illusions about that.

'I'll see what I can do.' Mr Collins hung up.

Beaming, Tom handed the rider back to Violet. 'And that is how you deal with ungrateful, self-important, egotistical teenage stars.'

'By threatening to expose them in the press as terrible people?' Violet, for some reason, didn't look quite as pleased with his victory as Tom thought she should.

'By making them aware of the truth of their situation,' he replied. 'They're public figures, and their attitudes and behaviour are noted. Don't you think the world should know that she wanted a bottle of three-thousand-dollar vodka more than she wanted to help the charity she was supposed to be appearing for?'

'No. Yes.' Frustration crossed Violet's face. 'Look, the point is, I didn't need you to save me. I could have dealt with it myself.'

'I'm sure you could.' Something told him this might be the time to tread gently. 'But sometimes these guys react better to the press than to...' Hell, now he was stuck. How to describe her in a way that wouldn't make her fly off the handle?

'Some girl who's only famous for who her parents are and for getting naked on the internet?' Bitterness filled Violet's voice as she quoted Mr Collins.

'Okay, I definitely wasn't going to say *that*.'

'But it's what you were thinking, right?' Violet gave him a sad smile. 'I know how people see me.'

The disappointment on her face made her look more fragile than he'd imagined she could, especially after their explosive first meeting in the airport. This wasn't a woman who revelled in her notoriety, who defended her mistakes and delighted in the press coverage. This wasn't the woman he'd watched—very briefly, before embarrassment got the better of him—in that sex tape.

'Does that happen a lot?' he asked, suddenly furious at the idea that it wasn't just one stupid man belittling Violet, but a whole host of them.

'Mr Collins?' She shrugged. 'Sometimes. I don't… Mostly, I'm not around people like that, so it's fine. If we're at a charity event or something, usually people won't say it to my face. But I hear the snickers and see the smiles, you know? I guess it's the only thing I'm famous for, so it's all anyone wants to talk about.'

'But it's not all that you are.' It surprised him how strongly he believed that—and how ashamed he felt that, when he'd arrived, he'd probably thought the same. What had changed?

'Was this why you didn't want to be in charge of the Benefit Concert?' he asked.

'I do want to do it,' she snapped. 'But…it's why my parents were worried about me doing it, yeah.' Her hands were busy playing with some stress toy she'd found in Rose's drawer when they were sorting the study—a globe that she could stretch and squeeze. After less than a week, it already looked considerably more worn than when they'd discovered it. 'They know I don't enjoy dealing with people so much these days. That was always left to Rose, really.'

These days. Since the sex tape? Tom frowned. Since

then, she'd stopped trusting anyone outside her immediate family, and avoided other people as much as possible.

Huh. Perhaps the stories he'd read when researching Violet Huntingdon-Cross weren't all there was to know. And he was a reporter—he always wanted to get to the truth, the real story.

Standing up, Tom reached across the desk and rescued the poor battered globe from between her fingers. 'Come on.' He took her hand and pulled her to her feet.

'What? Where are we going?' That puzzled frown line between her eyebrows was actually kind of cute, Tom decided.

'Lunch,' he told her. 'Completely off the record. I promise.'

It quickly emerged that Tom had no idea where they could actually go for lunch. 'Hey, you live here,' he said. 'Where's good?'

Rolling her eyes, Violet grabbed her handbag and car keys. 'Come on.'

As she started the engine, and tried to ignore Tom fiddling with the radio, she weighed up her options. There was the Peacock in the village, but that was just across the road from the church and the vicar's favourite afternoon haunt. She could almost guarantee that having lunch there with Tom would mean that the whole flower committee would be talking about her again by Sunday. There was the Three Tuns in the next village over, but Mum and her ladies sometimes took lunch there mid-week, and Violet couldn't remember if it was one of those days. Even if Mum wasn't there, the ladies might be.

So that left the Fox and Hounds, three villages over and with hand-cut chips to die for. Violet felt she could live with that.

'Is there any reason we're crossing county lines to grab a sandwich?' Tom asked as they drove past the turning for the village.

'Hand-cut chips,' Violet replied. It was only a partial lie, at least.

'Fair enough.' Tom settled back into his seat, the radio playing something obscure and jazzy, and folded his hands behind his head.

'So, these questions you want to ask…' It made Violet a little nervous, how relaxed he was. As if he already knew the answers to the things he was going to ask.

'When we get to the pub.' Were his eyes closed? Violet snapped her gaze away from the road ahead just long enough to check. Yep, he was half asleep in her car. Again.

'Okay, but you know I don't believe in off the record, right? I distinctly remember having that conversation.' That too revealing, too intimate conversation. Since then, she'd taken care to keep their interactions to a minimum. When he'd stopped by to see if he could help with the Benefit Concert a few days ago, she'd handed him a call sheet and left him to it. And when he'd been helping her sort the study, it had been easy to just boss him around.

Until today. Violet was under no illusions who was in charge today, even if she was the one holding the steering wheel. And she really didn't like it.

Beside her, Tom sighed, brought his hands down to rest in his lap and opened his eyes. 'Okay, look. This is how this is going to work. We are going to have lunch. Over lunch, we will make friendly conversation. We will probably talk about our families, our friends, our lives. Because that's what people do when they go out for lunch.'

'Not always,' Violet interjected. 'When we have flower committee lunches we mostly talk about other people. In fact, most lunches I've ever been to have been filled with people talking about other people.' Seemed people were always more comfortable gossiping about people they barely knew than about themselves. In fact, they especially seemed to like talking about her, she'd found.

'Fair point,' Tom conceded. 'Okay, then, imagine we're at some sort of internet dating meet-up thing.'

Violet couldn't help but laugh. 'No way.'

'Why not?'

'Because no logical computer programme in the world would ever put us together!' The journalist and the woman who got screwed over—quite literally and in front of millions—by one. Not a natural match.

'You don't know that!' Tom twisted in his seat to grin at her. 'We're both relatively young, relatively attractive...'

Violet tossed her hair over her shoulder, the way her mum did when she was dealing with idiots who didn't know they were idiots. 'Relatively?'

'In your case, relative to the pop stars and supermodels of this world. In mine...relative to everyone else.' Tom shrugged, as if to admit he knew the argument was kind of weak.

Violet raised her eyebrows as she pulled into the car park of the Fox and Hounds.

'Regardless of our relative attractiveness levels, I can assure you that our personality profiles would be very, very different.' Violet switched off the engine.

'Oh, I think we could have stuff in common.'

'How would you know? You don't know the first thing about me, apart from what you've read on the internet.' And watched, of course, although she didn't feel the need to remind him of that.

'Exactly.' Tom flashed her a grin and opened the door. 'And you don't know anything about me.'

'Except that you're a reporter.'

'That's my job, not who I am.' He got out of the car.

'So who are you then?' Violet called after him.

'Come to lunch and find out.' Tom leant down, rested him arms on the door frame and peered in at her. 'I'll do you a deal. For every question you answer of mine, I'll answer one of yours. Off the record.'

'I told you, I don't believe in that.'

'You might by the end of lunch. Now come on. I'm starving.'

CHAPTER NINE

VIOLET HAD BEEN RIGHT—the hand-cut chips were definitely worth the trip. The conversation, not so much. So far, over a pint of bitter for him and an orange juice for her, they'd discussed the menu, the merits of starters over puddings and the general preference for both, whether a table by the window might be nicer than one by the bar, and if the couple arguing in the car park were ever coming in.

But now, as the waitress retreated after leaving them their meals, he had his chance.

'So, do you want to go first, or shall I?' Tom popped another chip in his mouth while Violet considered her answer. Then, since it seemed to be taking her a while, he ate another. 'That wasn't meant to be such a brainteaser, you know.'

'It's a big decision!' Violet said. 'Like that bit in *The Princess Bride* with the iocane powder. You know… *Are you the sort of person who'd put poison in your glass or my glass?* That bit.' She looked down and selected her own chip, biting it in half.

'How, exactly, is lunch with me like deciding whether to drink poison or not?'

'Not lunch. The question thing,' Violet said. 'I mean, if you ask first, then I'll know the sort of level of questions we're asking, which makes it easier for me to come

up with mine. But if I go first, then I can see how good
your answers are before deciding how good *my* answers
should be. See?'

'Sure.' Or, you know, not at all. 'So, you like movies?'
Tom asked, oddly charmed by her uncertainty.

Violet's gaze flew up to meet his. 'Is that your first
question? Because I hadn't decided…'

'Okay. Not an official question. Just an idle wondering.'
Anything that got her talking was good with him.

'Then, yes. I like movies.' She took a breath. 'So, my
turn.'

'You've decided, then?'

Violet nodded. 'I think so.'

'So was that me going first, or did that one not count
and this next question is you going first?' He grinned at
the frustration that crossed her face.

'Does it matter?'

'Not really, I suppose.' Tom settled back in his chair.
'Go on, then. Ask away.'

'Why did you agree to come and stay at Huntingdon
Hall, and work on this book for Dad?'

Was that an easy one, to lull him into a false sense of
security? Or did she just have no idea what to ask? Either
way, he wasn't going to be so gentle.

'Because it's the chance of a lifetime,' he said with a
shrug. Faint disappointment coloured Violet's face, and
he realised suddenly that maybe this wasn't an easy question. Maybe she was asking more than he'd first thought.
He paused, and considered the real answer. 'The Screaming Lemons were my mum's favourite band; they were
the soundtrack to my childhood. So even if this wasn't a
great opportunity to really make my name—and hopefully some money—I'd still have wanted to take the job.
Your dad, his friends, your family—you're part of mod-

ern history. You matter to the collective memory of music lovers everywhere. I don't want that to be lost when we're all dead and gone.'

'The music would live on,' Violet said, her head tipped slightly to one side as she studied him. 'Isn't that enough?'

'In lots of ways, yes. But the Lemons were more than just the music. They're people too—people who mean a lot to their fans, like my mother. And I don't want the truth of who they are to be lost to the stories and anecdotes of people who barely knew them.' Had he even realised why this mattered to him until she'd asked? He didn't think so. Until this moment, he'd thought he was just there to do a job—a fun, fulfilling and hopefully lucrative job, but a job nonetheless. Now it felt more like a vocation.

'So is your mum pleased you're doing it?' Violet asked.

'That's a separate question,' Tom pointed out with a frown. Why had he even mentioned his mother? She was the last thing he wanted to talk about, and he had put the idea in her head. He was normally sharper than this. 'My turn first.'

Violet took a deep breath, as if steeling herself for something deeply unpleasant. 'Go on, then.'

What to ask? Or, rather, what to ask first? He had a lengthy list in his head of things he wanted to know, but where to start? If he went in with something too heavy, she might shy away. But if he started out gentle and they ran out of time, or she called a halt earlier than he'd like, he might never get to the important questions. Tricky.

In the end, he went for something in the middle.

'How do you feel about your twin sister marrying your best friend?'

Violet rolled her eyes and picked up her sandwich with both hands. 'I wondered how long it would take you to get to that.' She took a bite of her sandwich—a stalling tactic,

Tom decided. Something to make her look busy while she considered her answer.

'You promised me the truth,' he reminded her.

Violet swallowed her mouthful. 'I know, I know. Okay, it's a little bit weird, but I'm honestly really happy for them. I thought I was going to have to spend the rest of my life pretending to like Will's fiancées, then celebrating when he inevitably ran off and left them at the altar. This time, I was praying for him to go through with it. They're a good match.'

'So why is it weird?' Tom asked, hoping she wouldn't notice him slipping in the extra question.

Violet tilted her head to the side, considering. 'I guess just because it was never like that with us. Rose is practically my double, but there's a chemistry and a connection between them that just never existed between me and Will. And now it's my turn again.'

She smiled, her gaze catching his, and Tom found himself mesmerised by those bright blue eyes once more. He knew what she meant about the chemistry. He'd met Rose, had a very pleasant lunch and conversation with her. But he'd never found himself wanting to uncover all her secrets, or wanting to reach across and tuck a rogue strand of hair behind her ear. If Rose had told him that no dating agency in the world would set them up, he'd have laughed with her—not stubbornly set out to prove her wrong.

Which was ridiculous. Violet was right—they had nothing in common, no shared history or world. So why was he trying so hard to find a connection between them? Even he wasn't oblivious enough to pretend it was just for a story.

'Go on, then,' he said, breaking away from the look first. 'Ask.'

'I already have. Is your mum pleased you're doing this story?' Violet asked, and Tom's gaze flew away from hers.

'Sorry, only…you mentioned her before—that she was a big fan of Dad's. I just wondered if you were close, I guess.'

'She's dead,' Tom said, wincing at how blunt it came out. 'I mean, she died, about seven years ago now. So, uh, she doesn't know I'm here, but if she did…yeah, I think she'd be pleased. I think she'd have wanted to come too!'

'I'm sorry.' Violet's eyes were wide and sad. 'The way you talked about her, I just assumed… It must have been awful.'

Tom shrugged. 'It was. Still is, in lots of ways. I miss her, of course. And I think about her a lot. But…' Did he want to tell her this? One confidence in the hope of winning a lot more from her in return. 'When she died…we weren't on the best of terms. That's what I regret most. Not having the time to make things right with her before she died.'

He'd expected the sympathy in Violet's eyes, but not the sadness. 'I really am sorry, Tom. But I think she must have known how much you loved her—I can tell just from five minutes speaking with you, and she knew you your whole life.'

'I hope so.' Tom reached for his pint as a distraction. 'My turn. So…' This was it. This was his chance to ask the question he really wanted to know the answer to, while she was still feeling sorry for him. So why didn't he want to ask it, all of a sudden?

He pushed himself to, though. 'The sex tape. Why did you never issue a statement about it? An apology or an explanation?'

'Because it was nobody's damn business,' Violet snapped. 'If they want to watch it, fine, I can't stop them. But I don't have to acknowledge it.'

'Yeah, but a leaked sex tape… There's always talk that the subject might have put it out themselves. For the publicity or whatever. You didn't even deny that.' And *every-body* denied that. That was what made the whole Sex Tape Twin scandal so strange.

Violet looked him straight in the eye, her mouth hard and her jaw tight. 'Since I didn't even know I was being filmed at the time, it seems unlikely that I'd have been able to leak it to the media, doesn't it?'

'You didn't…you honestly didn't know you were being filmed?' Because that made it a whole different story. That…well, that explained a lot about why Violet was so touchy on the subject of trust.

'Of course I didn't! Do you really think I'd let someone film me doing…that?' She shook her head. 'Of course you do. Because you don't know me at all, just like I said. All you know about me is what you've read on the internet, the same as everyone else. Despite the fact you've spent the last week in my home—and apparently learnt nothing at all.'

'I didn't… I just assumed…' His arguments sounded stupid now. Of course Violet wouldn't—this was the woman who trusted no one outside her family. Why would she trust someone to film her being that vulnerable? Except, of course, something had to have happened to make her that wary. And it would make sense for this to be it. 'You looked straight into the camera, Violet. You had to know it was there.'

She blinked at him, shock in those blue eyes. 'I…I did? God, how many times did you watch it, Tom?'

'Not even once all the way through,' he promised. 'But there are stills…'

'Oh, I know. Someone sent a whole pack of them to my parents, along with a note that read "Your daughter is a whore" in bright red lipstick.'

'That's…wow. That's awful.'

'Yeah.' Reaching over, Violet stole his pint and took a sip. Then she sighed. 'Okay, look. I will tell you the story of the sex tape saga. But then that's it for today, yeah? And if you use *any* of it in this damn book of yours—'

'I should. You should want me to,' Tom interrupted. 'The world thinks that you filmed that tape on purpose. Half of them probably think you leaked it yourself. That's all the world knows of you. Don't you want them to know the truth?'

'I just want them all to forget,' Violet whispered, and something in Tom's chest clenched tight at the misery in her voice.

'Tell me what happened,' he said, reaching across the table to take her hand.

Violet looked up, her eyes wide and sad, and said, 'Okay.'

Oh, God, she didn't want to talk about this. Didn't want to admit all over again how stupid she'd been. Stupid, naïve and blind. Or, as Rose put it, nineteen.

'So, after I left boarding school, I took a gap year. I did some work experience at a newspaper because I thought I wanted to study journalism.'

'*You* wanted to become a reporter? You?'

Violet rolled her eyes at the mocking disbelief on Tom's face.

'Yes. I was eighteen then, and a totally different person. And this will go a lot quicker if you don't question everything.' If he interrupted her too much, Violet wasn't sure she could get through to the end of the story at all.

'Sorry. Carry on.' Tom took a big bite of his burger to show he wasn't going to talk any more.

'Okay, so I was working on this paper where no one cared who my parents were—or if they did, it was mostly only to complain about it. I wasn't getting paid, and mostly I fetched coffee, made photocopies and—eventually, once they realised I wasn't an idiot—checked copy and wrote filler pieces from press releases that got emailed in.'

'Sounds familiar,' Tom said through a mouthful of lunch.

'While I was there, I met a guy.'

'Less familiar.'

Violet tried to smile, to acknowledge his attempt to lighten the mood. But just thinking back to those days made her chest hurt. She'd been so young, so carefree. She'd really believed she could do anything she wanted, could be anyone if she just worked at it hard enough.

Finding out she was wrong had almost broken her.

'He was called Nick. He was one of the paper's senior reporters and he kind of took me under his wing. At first I thought it might be because of who my parents were— even then, I was used to people trying to get close to me just so they could get closer to *them*. But Nick didn't seem interested in them. Only me.' He'd made her feel so special—as if her family were the least interesting thing about her. No one had ever managed that before.

Of course, it was all a lie, which might have made it easier.

'What happened?' Tom's expression was already grim, knowing how the story ended. Violet didn't blame him. It wasn't pretty.

'We dated for a bit. He took me places I'd never even thought of going before. I thought...' So, so naïve. 'I thought it was something real. That he loved me as much as I believed I loved him.'

'But he didn't?' There was no pity in Tom's eyes, which she appreciated. The pity was almost worse than the laughter.

'He filmed us in bed together without my knowledge, then put it out on the internet. I believe he also sold some of the photos to the highest bidder first.'

'Bastard.' Violet had never heard quite so much vehemence put into two syllables before.

'The worst thing was…it took me a while to realise what he'd done. I thought it was a fake, or that someone had filmed us without our knowledge…' She swallowed, not wanting to relive the next part. But she'd promised him the truth. 'I went to see him, talking about lawyers and what we could do to get it taken down…and he laughed at me. As did the woman who was in his bed at the time.'

Tom winced at that. 'Jesus. That's…what a piece of work. No wonder you've been hiding out at Huntingdon Hall for the last eight years.'

Violet shrugged. 'It's safe there. I don't have to deal with the press, or the public, or what everyone thinks they know about me, most of the time.'

'So…that's when you stopped trusting people?'

'Do you blame me?' Violet asked.

Tom shook his head. 'No. But one thing I don't understand. Why didn't you let people know the truth? Put out a statement, or sue the scumbag?'

Rose had wanted her to, Violet remembered. Had wanted her to fight back, to fight as dirty as Nick had. She'd wanted to use every connection their parents had to ruin Nick's life the way he'd wrecked hers.

But Violet had said no.

'I didn't want to be that person,' she said, wondering if Tom would understand. Rose had, eventually, but it had taken years. 'I didn't want to drag things out in the papers and on the news. I didn't want to make things all about me. I just wanted it to go away. For people to forget.'

'Except they never did,' Tom said.

Violet stared down at her plate. 'No. They didn't. And it's too late now to change anyone's ideas about me.'

'Maybe not.' Tom leant back in his chair, studying her so intently that it made Violet's skin itch.

'What do you mean?'

Tom shrugged. 'I just wondered if maybe your dad's determination to have me write this book, now, might have something to do with telling the truth about your story, too. Letting the world know what really happened at last.'

Violet shook her head. It wasn't enough. 'Why would they believe it? It's too late now, anyway. It's much harder to change entrenched beliefs than just telling the truth.'

Tom's smile was slow and full of promise. 'Then you clearly haven't read much of my writing. Just wait and see what I can do.'

CHAPTER TEN

'SO, WHERE DO you want to start today?' Rick Cross lounged back in his chair in the little sitting room off his studio, looking utterly relaxed. A complete contrast to how his daughter had looked when Tom had asked *her* a few innocent questions over lunch at the start of the week.

Focus, Tom. He had *the* Rick Cross here ready to interview, and he did not have time to be distracted by thoughts of Violet.

'Well, we've covered the basic history of the band—although there are lots of areas I want to dig deeper into later, when we have more time. But since I know you need to head out again in an hour...maybe we should use the time to talk about where The Screaming Lemons are today, and where they're headed next?'

'And the family. Don't forget that,' Rick said. 'I want the story of my family to be told, as much as the band. And it's exciting times around here at the moment.'

'Of course.' Including, presumably, Violet's story. How did she feel about that? he wondered. On the one hand, it would mean everyone knowing the truth—and hadn't he promised her he'd change the minds of the Great British—and American—public with his words? But even if the new press attention was more positive than it had ever been before, it would still put her front and centre again. And leave people talking about her sex life more than ever.

From what he'd learned of Violet, that wasn't going to go down well.

'But let's start with the band,' Tom said. He wanted to talk to Violet some more himself before he started discussing her with her father.

Rick gave him a knowing look. 'Okay. What do you want to know?'

Tom already had every detail of the upcoming tour and album launch, what singles they were planning to release when, who'd written most of which song, and who'd done the cover art—and nothing that he couldn't have got from an informative press release.

He needed to go deeper.

'What issues did you run into writing and recording this album that you maybe haven't had to worry about before?' he asked.

Rick smirked. 'You mean broken hips and playing the guitar with a walking frame now we're all so old?'

'Not necessarily.' Tom gave him an apologetic smile. 'But your last album was five years ago now, and life has to have changed for you all. Two of your daughters have got married, your first grandchild is on the way... Jez got divorced a couple of years ago, right?' Rick nodded. 'And the world—the music scene particularly—has changed too. How did that affect things?'

Leaning back in his chair, Rick brought one ankle up to rest on his opposite knee, obviously belying the need for hip replacements. He was only sixty, if that, Tom thought. There was a lot more music to come from the Lemons yet.

'I think...the music scene changes by the minute. You can't write songs to that. I let the marketing people worry about it, and we just get on with writing the best tunes we can. As for the family stuff… Every year we become more settled, happier in the place we're in. We're fortunate. We're all healthy, living the lives we want to live.' An uncomfortable look crossed his face and Tom knew he couldn't *not* ask any more.

'Except Violet,' he said softly.

'Except my Violet,' Rick confirmed.

Tom put down his notepad on the low table between them, dropping his pen on top of it. His phone was still recording, of course, but he knew he wouldn't use whatever Rick said next. Not officially, anyway.

'Is that one of the reasons you asked me here?'

Rick raised an eyebrow. 'You think you can make Violet happy? Get her to follow her dreams at last?'

'Not that.' Tom shook his head, hoping he wasn't actually blushing in front of a rock legend. As if he'd be so presumptuous as to think he could fix Violet's life. 'I meant…the world never got to hear the true story. Their image of Violet, their beliefs about her—that's a large part of what keeps her hiding away here. It did cross my mind that you might want this book to change that. To let people see the real Violet.'

Rick studied him for a long moment before answering, and Tom fought his impulse to look away. He had a feeling that this moment in time, this answer, would set the tone for every interview that followed. That Rick was judging him and his abilities right now, making a decision about how much to tell him—for this question and every one that came after.

And Tom really, really wanted to be found worthy.

'I think, in the end, that Violet will be the one to show the world what she's really made of. She'll be the one to stand up and say, *You were wrong about me.*' Rick flashed a quick smile. 'But anything you can do to help that along would be appreciated.'

Violet glared at the piece of paper in front of her as the phone in her hand clicked over to voicemail again.

'You've reached Jake Collins, music agent. You know what to do at the beep.'

She hung up. If Olivia's manager hadn't responded to any of the other messages she'd left him in the days since their last phone call, not to mention the emails, then why would this message be any different?

Maybe she should threaten him, like Tom had. Except she was very afraid that Mr Collins would just laugh at her and go right back to ignoring her. Not ideal.

Placing her phone back on the desk, she read through Olivia's contract to appear in the concert again. That, at least, was signed. But since she'd somehow got a clause included that meant it was only valid with the accompanying agreed and signed rider, it wasn't worth the paper it was printed on. The rider was not only unsigned, but nowhere near agreed.

Violet had emailed over a revised version after their last conversation, deleting the request for ridiculously over-priced vodka amongst other things, and leaving in the more reasonable stuff. Since then, she'd heard nothing from Olivia's camp.

A knock on the door roused her from her thoughts and she looked up to see Tom loitering in the doorway. She scowled at him by reflex.

'What did I do to put such a look on your face today?' he asked good-naturedly, dropping to sit in what Violet had somehow come to think of as his chair. 'Since you haven't actually seen me since breakfast, when I think I was mostly inoffensive.'

'Jake Collins isn't answering my calls. Or my emails.'

'Olivia's manager?' Tom shook his head. 'He likes his games, that one.'

'I'd rather figured that out for myself, actually,' Violet snapped. 'And this particular game is down to you, I think.'

'You think he's ignoring you because of what I said to him the other day?' Tom shrugged. 'He still deserved it.'

Which was true, but not particularly helpful. 'I think he's stringing me along, making me fret until the very last moment when he'll show up with both the signed rider and my big name act for the concert.'

'Then why are you worrying?' Tom asked. 'Just ignore his little mind games and get on with everything else.'

He made it sound so easy. 'Because there's always the possibility that he's playing a different game. Olivia's contract is pretty much meaningless without the signed rider and if they pull out at the last minute, once all the concert publicity is done and the programmes printed…'

Tom winced at the implication. 'So what are you going to do?'

And wasn't that the three thousand dollar bottle of vodka question? What did she do? Keep phoning and emailing like a desperate person? The ballsy thing to do would be to cancel Olivia altogether, unless the rider was signed by the end of the day—Violet was sure that was what Rose would do. But Violet didn't have Rose's connections to help her find a suitably starry replacement at the last moment.

Which only left door number three.

'I'm going to go and find Jake Collins and his teenage pop idol and get a signature on this bloody rider, that's what I'm going to do.' Violet wished she felt as confident as she sounded. Turning her laptop so Tom could see, she elaborated. 'Olivia's in the middle of a UK arena tour at the moment. Today's Friday, so she's in...' she ran a finger down the list of tour dates on the screen '...Brighton. So that's where I'm going.'

Tom blinked at her, then a slow smile spread across his face. 'Road trip. Cool. When do we leave?'

'We?' That wasn't the plan at all. 'No we. Just me. I need to do this myself.'

'Hey, I'm not planning on interfering,' Tom said, holding his hands up in a surrender pose. 'I just want to see you take Jake Collins down yourself this time. Off the record, of course.'

'Of course,' Violet echoed with disbelief. As much as, oddly, she found she wouldn't mind Tom's company on the trip, she wasn't sure this was an episode she wanted finding its way into his book.

'Besides, I know the PR staff at the venue. I can probably get us press credentials to get us into the gig in the first place.'

Okay, now that would be useful. She hadn't even thought beyond getting to Brighton to how she'd actually get past security to see the star and her manager.

Decision made, Violet closed the lid of her laptop. 'Better grab your stuff then. If I want to get there before the gig, I need to leave in...' she checked her watch '...twenty minutes.'

Tom grinned and jumped to his feet. 'I'll be ready in fifteen.'

Which was all very well for him. Violet wasn't sure she'd ever be ready for a road trip with Tom Buckley.

CHAPTER ELEVEN

TOM WAS ALREADY leaning against the car when Violet emerged from Huntingdon Hall eighteen minutes later, overnight bag in hand. He hadn't wanted to risk her disappearing without him.

Inviting himself along on her little road trip had been a spur of the moment decision, but he'd decided while packing that it was a good one. From a purely professional standpoint, watching Violet take on Jake Collins could be pure gold for the book—not to mention the fact that a couple of hours trapped in a car together would give him plenty of time to interview her on the way to Brighton. For once, she wouldn't be able to escape his questions.

He was less comfortable with his other reasons for wanting to accompany her. Because he had to admit the truth—to himself, if not to Violet—that when he'd made the decision to join her he hadn't been thinking professionally at all. He'd been thinking about the look on her face when Jake Collins had spoken to her as if she were nothing. He'd been thinking about her plucking up the courage to face him and demand a signature.

He'd been thinking that he didn't want her to have to do it alone. And he wasn't sure he wanted to know why it mattered so much to him that he would be there to protect her.

Shaking his head to clear his rebellious thoughts, Tom grinned at Violet as she drew close. 'Ready?'

'As I'll ever be.' She gave him a less certain smile. 'You know, you really don't have to come. I'll be fine.'

Tom shrugged. 'I know. But I've been in the country for over a week now, and still haven't seen anything but the airport and Huntingdon Hall. I'm ready for a road trip.'

Violet opened the trunk and they both stashed their bags. 'You've been to Britain before, though, right?' she asked as she slid into the driver's seat.

'Loads of times,' Tom admitted. 'But I've never seen any of it with you.'

She opened her mouth as if about to answer, then closed it again, frowning at the steering wheel. 'We should get going, then.'

Tom settled back into the passenger seat as Violet started the engine, turned on the radio and pulled out onto the long driveway. At least he wasn't the only one a little unsettled by their connection.

They travelled mostly in silence, content to listen to the radio, until they reached the motorway—and stationary traffic. Tom's only attempts at conversation—gentle precursors to the questions he actually wanted to ask—had been rebuffed by a sharp, 'I'm trying to concentrate on the road right now,' from Violet. Not that he believed her. He knew a stalling tactic when he heard one.

But as the motionless cars spread out ahead of them as they crested the slip road, he straightened up in his seat and prepared to try again.

'Looks like we might have to catch Olivia after her performance,' he said, as casually as he could.

Violet swore in response, and he hid a grin. Where had a nice girl like her learnt words like that?

'That was off the record, by the way,' she added.

'Of course,' Tom said, as seriously as he could manage.

'Dammit.' Violet thumped a hand against the steering wheel. 'Can you check the traffic reports? See how bad this is likely to be?'

Tom nodded and reached for his phone but, before he could find it, a shrill ringing filled the car.

'That's mine.' Violet nodded towards where her phone sat in a little space below the dashboard. Cars up ahead jerked forward, just enough for her to try and edge the car onto the main motorway. 'Is it Mr Collins?'

Tom fished out the phone and looked. 'It's your mother.'

'Of course.' Violet sighed. 'I'll call her back when we get there.'

'Or I could just…' Tom swiped the screen to answer, and gave Violet an innocent smile in response to her glare. 'Hello, Sherry. Violet's just driving at the moment. Can I help?'

'Tom, great—yes, please. Can you tell her that I just had Frances Littlewood on the phone, asking who Violet is bringing as her plus one for Henry's wedding next weekend? She says one of Henry's ushers is single if she's stuck…'

Sherry sounded harried, which was very unlike her. But then, Henry Littlewood's wedding was the theatre dynasty event of the summer. In fact, he had a feeling that Rick and Sherry were godparents to Henry himself. The Littlewoods had the same sort of money, prestige and power in the acting world as Rick and Sherry had in the music one. It was bound to be quite the event. Quite the *public* event. Just the sort of thing Violet usually avoided, as far as Tom could tell.

He covered the phone with his hand. 'She wants to know who you're taking to Henry Littlewood's wedding next weekend. Otherwise, Frances Littlewood is setting you up with an usher.'

Violet swore again and Tom grinned, glad Sherry couldn't hear.

'Not looking forward to it?' he asked, already pretty sure of the answer.

'Henry's a family friend, and his mother made his fiancée make me one of her bridesmaids too, which she probably hates me for.' Violet sighed. 'I want to go for him, and Mum and Dad will be there, probably Daisy and Seb too… It's just…'

'You don't want to face all the people. And the cameras.'

'Yeah.'

Tom considered. There was a chance Violet might never forgive him for what he was about to do. On the other hand, if he could convince her of the truth—that it was the act of a friend, that he honestly had no ulterior motive for this… maybe it could bring them closer.

Maybe, one day, Violet would learn to trust him.

He lifted the phone to his ear again.

'Sherry, if it's okay with you and Rick, I'm going to accompany Violet. As her date, not a reporter on this occasion!'

'Well,' Sherry said, sounding taken aback, 'that sounds lovely. I'm sure we'll all have a delightful day.'

'Me too.' Although, judging by the shocked glare on Violet's face, only if he lived that long. 'See you later, Sherry.'

Silence reined in the motionless car for a long, long moment.

Then Violet said, 'You are never answering my phone again.'

What was he thinking? Well, actually, Violet was pretty sure she knew exactly what he was thinking—what a perfect way to further his career by sneaking into a society wedding under the guise of being her date. It wasn't as if she hadn't got used to being used for her name and family over the years, but this one really did take the biscuit.

'I meant what I said,' Tom told her, his expression deceptively earnest. 'I'm not going to the wedding as a journalist.'

'No, you said you were going as my date. Aren't you supposed to *ask* a girl before declaring something a date?' Because if he'd asked she could have said no. And she almost certainly would have. Probably.

'Well, it was kind of a spur of the moment decision. Much like this road trip.' He shot her a sideways glance she pretended not to see. 'Is it such a bad idea?'

'Yes!'

'Why?'

'Because...oh, so many reasons. Because you're not my boyfriend; you're the guy who's here to research and write about me and my family. Because you're always, always a reporter, no matter how much you pretend you're taking a day off. Journalists don't do off-duty.'

'Okay, answer me this one question honestly.' Violet stared out of the windscreen at the road as he talked. Because she needed to concentrate on driving, not because she was ignoring him. Really. Even if the car wasn't moving. 'Will the wedding be more or less fun with me there to keep you company?'

Damn him. Violet bit the inside of her cheek to keep from answering. Even with Daisy and her parents there, it would be better with Tom. Because Daisy and Seb would be all loved-up again, and so would Mum and Dad probably, and everyone would start telling stories about their own weddings or engagements or romantic moments... and, for once, she wouldn't have to sit there as sorry single Violet whose heart had been betrayed and broken by the only man she'd ever loved.

'Violet? More or less fun?' Tom pressed.

'More.' The word came out begrudgingly.

'Great! Then it's all settled.' Tom beamed at her and Violet almost missed her chance to move forward two metres.

Settled wasn't the word she'd use at all. In fact, things felt more unsettled than ever to Violet.

'So, how many times will you have been a bridesmaid this year, after this one?' Tom asked.

Violet tried to pretend her cheeks weren't getting warm. 'Three, including Mum and Dad's renewal. And you know what they say...'

'No idea, actually,' Tom said cheerfully.

'Three times the bridesmaid, never the bride,' Violet quoted. 'Of course, this is actually the sixteenth time I've been a bridesmaid, so I think we're long past worrying about that.' Not that that would stop everyone there thinking it, or whispering it behind her back, she was sure.

Tom let out a low whistle. 'Sixteen. That's, wow. A lot.'

'Yeah. Most of them were as kids—you know, family friends or people who just wanted cute, famous twin girls to walk down the aisle with them or to make sure Rick and Sherry were photographed at their wedding. You know how it goes.'

'Yeah, I guess.'

'I've only done it five or six times since I left university. Mostly for friends.' Why was she still talking about this? He couldn't possibly care.

'Still, it's a good job you look so great in bridesmaid dresses,' Tom said with a grin.

No pretending she wasn't blushing this time. But thinking about bridesmaid dresses just made her remember the one she was wearing when she'd met him, and what had followed next.

Still not her finest moment.

'Did you check that traffic report?' she asked, eager for a change of subject.

Tom pulled out his own phone and jabbed at the screen for a while. 'Okay, it looks like this carries on for the next couple of junctions. Then we should be clear.'

Violet sighed. 'So, after the gig it is. There's no way we'll make it before at this rate.' They'd been cutting it close as it was. And by the time the gig was over she was going to be exhausted, even if things went well.

'Want me to see if I can find us rooms at a hotel somewhere near the arena?' Tom asked, as if he'd read her mind. It was kind of disconcerting.

She bit her lip. Did she? It would mean a whole night away with Tom Buckley, plus the drive home tomorrow. He was bound to use that to his advantage, even if she was slightly reassured by his use of the plural 'rooms'. But was that more dangerous than driving home exhausted? No. Of course it wasn't.

She sighed. 'Yeah, I guess so.'

They inched forward another few metres as Tom frowned at his phone screen. Eventually he gave a little cheer of triumph, and tucked his phone away again.

'Got something?'

'Nothing near the arena,' Tom said, 'but I got us two rooms right on the front, in some hotel with an old-fashioned name. I'm not sure I've ever seen the ocean in Britain.'

'It's the sea here,' Violet corrected him. 'And the British seaside is an institution, I suppose. You should see it.'

A broad smile split Tom's face. 'Great! Only thing I

can't figure out is why one of the rooms was half the price
of the other.'

Violet could guess. Not all of those old seaside hotels
were in the best of repair these days. 'Well, tell you what,
you can take that room and find out. Okay?'

Tom's smile didn't even fade an iota. 'Whatever you
say, boss.'

Violet turned her attention back to the traffic ahead of
her. She had a feeling it was going to be a very long night.

CHAPTER TWELVE

THE CONCERT HAD to be well underway by the time Violet swung her little car into the car park nearest to the arena. Tom had exercised discretion as the better part of valour and avoided asking too many questions for the latter part of the journey, as Violet's expression grew stony and set as the traffic worsened.

He almost pitied Jake Collins, the mood she was in. But only almost.

'You can definitely get us in there, yes?' Violet asked, switching off the engine and lights. At high summer, the sun was still going down but it still felt late.

'It's done.' Tom stretched his legs out of the door, feeling his back pop as he arched it. 'There should be passes waiting for us at the door.' He didn't mention exactly how much favour currency he'd exchanged for that privilege.

Violet stalked off in what he presumed was the direction of the arena and he hurried to catch her up, pausing only briefly to admire the look of her determined walk and her behind in tight blue jeans.

As he'd promised, they were waved through backstage without any noticeable delays. From the amused look one of the security guards gave Violet, Tom had a feeling that she could probably have talked her way in there without him anyway. She had a very famous face, after all. Not to mention the rest of her.

Violet paused for a moment in the empty corridor backstage as they approached the star dressing room. The sound of Olivia's latest hit echoed around the hallways. Tom stood beside her as she leant against the cool painted wall.

'You ready for this?' he asked, his voice low, relying on his close proximity to ensure he was heard.

'No.' She gave him a wobbly smile. 'But I'm going to do it anyway.'

God, you had to admire that kind of spirit. That kind of grit. The woman he'd thought she was when they met wouldn't have been afraid, and the one he'd come to know in his first days at Huntingdon Hall wouldn't have dared. But this Violet—the woman he was beginning to think of as his Violet, without any justification—she was braver than either of those other women he'd thought he knew.

She was magnificent.

'I'll be right here,' Tom promised. 'But you won't need me.'

Her smile firmed up a little at that, and something in his chest grew warmer. Was it his heart? It had been so long he could hardly tell.

Slowly, Tom leant forward to press a kiss against her forehead, but she tilted her head up to look at him and then...well, it was only natural for him to place that kiss on her lips, right?

'Yeah? Well, you tell them not to call me again until we're talking about top billing, okay? My girl headlines or nothing at all.'

The terse voice cut through what Tom thought was pretty much a perfect moment. Violet jerked back, putting unwelcome inches between them, and Tom bit back a growl of frustration.

'Mr Collins,' Violet said, in what Tom recognised as a dangerously sweet voice. Shaking off the kiss fog that had filled his brain, he tried to focus on what was happening in front of him. How much had the agent seen?

Jake Collins blinked, then jabbed at the screen of his smartphone and slipped it into his pocket. 'Miss Huntingdon-Cross. What a...surprise. And Mr Buckley, correct? Now, what can I do for you two lovebirds?'

Damn. That answered the question of whether Jake had noticed them kissing. Violet's cheeks grew a little pink and Tom cursed his lack of impulse control. Couldn't he have waited to kiss the girl *after* she'd taken care of business?

'I won't take more than a moment of your time, Mr Collins,' Violet continued smoothly, ignoring Jake's amused look and raised eyebrows. Tom stayed a few steps away to the side, close enough to see everything, but not so close that Jake Collins would be able to turn things round and try to deal with him instead. This was Violet's rodeo.

'We're actually in the middle of a pretty big gig here right now, in case you haven't noticed.' Jake's gaze flicked over to Tom. 'I realise you may have had other distractions to deal with.'

Again, Violet ignored the innuendo, so Tom resisted the urge to land a punch on the manager's face. Just.

'Trust me, Mr Collins, I'm here on business,' Violet said crisply. 'Olivia hasn't signed the revised rider yet. You may not be aware but the contract for her to appear at the Benefit Concert is void without the signed rider.' Jake's mouth twitched up at that. Of course he was aware. But Violet kept talking. 'Since I couldn't get hold of you by phone or email, I thought the simplest thing would be to come down here in person with the rider.' She pulled a folder out of her bag and handed it over.

Jake didn't even open it. 'Obviously you realise that

Olivia needs to sign this? And she's a little busy right now.'
As if to punctuate his statement, Olivia hit the high note
of her latest single and the walls around them vibrated
with the sound.

'We can wait.' Violet smiled patiently and Tom brought
his hand to his mouth to hide his own grin.

With a sigh, Jake flipped open the cover of the folder
and glared at the paper inside. 'This isn't what I agreed
with your sister.'

'That is the standard rider that every other act appearing in the concert has signed, plus a couple of the more
reasonable requests from Olivia's original list,' Violet said.
'If it isn't acceptable to you, or to Olivia, I need you to tell
me now. We have just over a week until the concert and if
I need to find a replacement I need to do it immediately.
I'm sure you understand.'

Tom glanced down at Violet's hands, resting at her
sides, and noticed they were trembling, just slightly. Jake
wouldn't have noticed, he was sure. No one who wasn't
looking, or who didn't know Violet, would. She sounded
completely in control of the moment, of the man even.

Only Tom knew she was terrified.

Had she been scared that night at the airport? He hadn't
known to look for the signs, then. Had just assumed that
she was the cocky, self-assured celebrity kid he was expecting.

Now he knew her better. And cared for her all the more
for it.

'You really think you could find an act of the same calibre as Olivia in a week?' Jake shook his head and laughed.

'It's not the calibre I'd be worried about,' Violet shot
back. 'The same level of fame may be a problem, but I
could call a dozen better acts and have them on the stage
in moments.' Tom winced at the sting in her words.

'Of course, the real problem would be the fans,' Jake threw back. 'Because, whatever you think of her talent, Olivia is the one they want to see. I'd like to see you fill that concert without her.'

Violet nodded, her face solemn. 'And I'm sure Olivia would hate to let down her fans. Which is why, if she's not planning to appear, it would be best to know now. So I can put out an official statement apologising to her fans on Olivia's behalf. I'm sure they'll understand when I explain that we were unable to divert enough money from the charity account to satisfy her. Especially when that information comes in a paragraph after a detailed description of all the good causes that money is used to support.' She looked thoughtful for a moment. 'Maybe I'll get Dad to put out the statement. After all, it's his concert, and his charities. We could include a list of all the acts who waived their fee for the concert altogether for comparison. What do you think?'

It was more or less the same threat Jake had made himself, but with more teeth. If Olivia pulled out now, Violet would eviscerate her reputation. Jake didn't want a diva on his books—even if that was what he had. He needed Olivia to appear wholesome and loving and giving, so the kids' mums would let their pre-teens buy her music.

Jake Collins glared at Violet for a long moment before flicking his gaze over to Tom. With a 'What can you do?' smile, Tom shrugged.

'Fine.' Jake snapped the word out as he flicked the folder closed again. 'I'll get her to sign it tonight and courier it to you tomorrow.'

'Perfect.' Violet's smile was sharp, with a hint of teeth. 'And if it's not with me by Monday, I'll issue that press release.' She held out a hand, which Jake took, obviously reluctantly. 'I'm so glad we were able to clear this up. I hope the rest of the tour goes well.'

Jake Collins turned on his heel and stalked away down the corridor without so much as a goodbye. Tom watched him go, aware Violet was doing the same. Then, once he'd disappeared around the corner, Tom let out a long breath.

'You did it,' he said.

'I really, really did.' Violet's eyes were wide, her expression stunned. 'I did it, all by myself.'

Tom grinned. 'So what now?'

The shock faded from Violet's face, replaced by elation. 'Now we celebrate!'

CHAPTER THIRTEEN

THE HOTEL BAR was mostly deserted, but Violet managed to scare up a barman to fetch them some drinks, while Tom carried their bags in from the car and got them checked in. She was glad of the few minutes alone; it gave her a chance to process everything that had happened since they'd arrived in Brighton. And somehow the confrontation with Jake Collins was fading in her memory, compared to the brief, soft, mesmerising kiss she'd shared with Tom beforehand.

But all too soon Tom was back and Violet found herself trying very hard not to stare at his mouth. Why had he kissed her? And was he planning on doing it again?

And if he wasn't, would she?

'Here's to beating that scumbag at his own game.' Tom raised his pint to Violet's glass of wine, and she dutifully chinked them together.

'You don't think I went too far?' Violet asked. After all, it was one thing to stop Jake Collins from trying to ruin her concert, another to behave just as badly to get her own way.

Tom shook his head. 'Trust me, I've seen too far. That was just far enough. Your sister would be proud.'

'Except we're not going to tell her about this, right?' Violet said. 'And it's definitely not going in your book.'

'But it's such a great story!' Tom protested.

'About me,' Violet replied. 'A story about me. And the book is supposed to be about the band, in case you've forgotten.'

'And your family. Your dad has been very specific about that.'

Violet rolled her eyes. 'I have no idea why. Him and Mum, yeah, I get. People want to read about their epic romance. And okay, maybe a tiny section on Daisy marrying into the aristocracy, or looking at all the work Rose has done with the band. But what is there to write about me except a sex scandal I'd much rather no one ever mentioned again?'

'I don't know,' Tom said. 'That's what I've been trying to find out.'

'By asking a thousand questions.'

'That you don't answer.' Tom raised his eyebrows. 'Why is that?'

God, he was unstoppable. 'I answered every question you asked me at lunch the other day. I told you everything you could possibly want to know.'

'About one bad experience with a guy eight years ago, yeah,' Tom said. 'But what about who you are now? What's happened in your life since? Your entire existence can't revolve around one bad sex tape, Violet.'

Except it did, however much it hurt to admit. 'Why does it matter so much to you that you know everything about my life?'

'Because I want to understand you!' Violet glanced around her to make sure no one else had come into the bar and started listening, but Tom obviously didn't care if they had. He was on a roll. 'Violet, you are a mystery to me. And uncovering mysteries is kind of my job.'

'But why do you care?' Violet whispered, knowing she

was really asking *Why did you kiss me?* and wishing she didn't need to know the answer so much. How had he got so cleanly under her skin? She'd only known the man a couple of weeks, but suddenly all she wanted in the world was to hear him say that she mattered to him.

'Because…because you're more than your past. You're…God, Violet, you could be anything you wanted, and you're hiding away at Huntingdon Hall. I want to understand you, to know the truth of you. I want…I want you to trust me.'

Didn't it always come down to that? Violet took a breath. 'I came here today, didn't I?'

'You did,' Tom admitted. 'And why was that? I mean, why did you take on the concert at all if you're not desperate to get back to doing *something* with your life?'

Why had she? It seemed so long ago already that she'd agreed to it. 'I think it was partly to prove a point to you,' she admitted. 'After we met at the airport… It felt like you thought I was nothing more than my parents' name and my own infamous internet appearance. I wanted to prove I was something more, I guess.'

'Good! Because you are. And I'm so damn glad you're starting to see it.' He took a long sip of his pint, then frowned. 'If that was only part of the reason, what was the rest?'

He was sitting too close to her to let her think straight. Violet wished she'd picked one of the other tables, one with two chairs on opposing sides, rather than this booth table with one long semi-circular seat. Here, he could keep sliding round until their legs were nearly touching and she couldn't concentrate on anything else…

A question. He'd asked her a question.

'I guess…I didn't want to let Rose down. Or my parents. And…'

'Yeah?' Another inch closer, and she could feel the length of his thigh against hers, warm and comforting. His arm was almost around her shoulders, resting on the back of the booth behind her, cocooning her, keeping her close and safe. Letting her know she could tell him her secrets.

'I wanted to do...more, I guess. I know you think I've just been hanging around at home, arranging the odd bouquet or something. And maybe that's what I wanted people to think, because then they wouldn't expect too much. I don't know.' She took a breath. This wasn't like her past, this was her life, and she wasn't ashamed of it—actually, she was pretty proud of it.

'I do a lot in our community, besides just the flowers, you know. I help out with pensioners' lunches at the church, I run a counselling group and...Mum and I, we set up a helpline. It's national, and it doesn't have our name on it anywhere. But we take calls from kids and teenagers who just need someone to talk to, or need help escaping from dangerous situations. I do a shift on the phones most days, and I take a lot of calls from teenage girls in their first relationships. Girls who've got in too far too fast and don't know how to get out again. I help them.'

She stopped, aware that Tom's hand was on her shoulder now and he was staring down at her, his eyes full of intensity and feeling she couldn't quite decipher.

'So, anyway. Not just sitting around arranging flowers,' she said. 'But I wanted to do more, and the concert... well, it wasn't about me, so it seemed like a safe way to try and do it.'

Tom shook his head. 'Every time I think I've got you sussed out, you go and surprise the hell out of me again and prove you're more than I could have even imagined.'

Violet stared up at him. 'Yeah?'

'Yeah.' Their gazes locked, and she knew before he dipped his head that he was going to kiss her again. And she wanted it so much...but something made her pull back.

'Wait,' she said, and hoped she wouldn't regret it for the rest of her life.

The woman was trying to kill him. That was all there was to it.

Swallowing hard, Tom backed up. Not too far—not far enough to let her forget that gorgeous chemistry that sizzled between them. Just enough for her to know that he wouldn't push anything until she was ready.

'What's the matter?' he asked, trying to find some rationality. But all he could think about was kissing her again, even when she'd made it very clear she didn't want that.

God, he was an idiot. What was he doing? Hell, what was he thinking? She was a subject. Not even that, the daughter of his subject. A secondary interest, worth about twenty pages in the book.

Not someone he should be falling for.

'I don't know.' Violet stared down at her hands, and Tom wished he could read her mind. 'I just...I'm not sure this is a good idea.'

Tom was. At least his body was damn certain it was the best idea he'd had in years.

'Why not?' he asked, disappointment clenching his chest even as he tried to fight it off. She was wary, he knew that. He just needed to win her over. Talk her round. It was all just words—and he was good at words. It was kind of his job, right?

'Because you're a reporter. Because I don't really do relationships. Because you're working for Dad. A million reasons.'

'None of which sound like you don't feel the same things I do when we're together.' She had to feel it too, right? No way that kind of connection only worked one way. It wasn't possible.

Violet sighed. 'Look, I'm not saying I'm not…that there isn't… Okay, fine. Yes, I'm attracted to you, even when I don't want to be. But that doesn't mean we need to…do anything about it. You're staying with my family, working with my parents… We can't risk screwing all that up.'

'It would be worth it.' He was damn sure of that. Even if she was only making the same arguments that had been buzzing round his head for days.

'Come on, Tom.' Violet's lips twisted up in a half smile. 'This is your big break. Don't tell me you'd be willing to risk that just for a quick tawdry fling with the Sex Tape Twin.'

'Don't say that,' Tom snapped. How could she still say that, after everything she'd just told him? 'That's not who you are. Not any more. And never to me.'

'I was, though. That was the first thing you knew about me. And the first thing I knew about you was that you'd watched that damn video.'

'It was work. I didn't…' God, there was no excuse here that would work, was there? 'You weren't…you to me then. You weren't Violet.'

Violet's smile was sad. 'But that's the point, isn't it? I'm not me to anyone. I'm just that stupid, naïve girl in a sexy video. I'm never just Violet.'

'You are to me now,' Tom promised.

'I hope so.' She looked up at him at last, blue eyes wide. 'But in lots of ways you're still just The Reporter to me. I don't…it's weird to think that I've opened up to you more than anyone since Will, but I still barely know anything about you.'

Well, that he could fix, surely? 'What do you want to know?'

'Everything,' Violet replied. 'But not tonight, I don't think. I need a little time to...process everything. I mean, I did something huge today, facing down Jake Collins. I couldn't have done that before, not even a month ago—I just froze up in front of people like that, knowing they were laughing at me inside. I'm changing, and I like it, and I think...I think a lot of it has to do with you being here. But it's all happening so fast, and I still have so much left to do for the concert, and...'

'You need time. I get that.' Disappointment warred with relief inside Tom. She wanted to know everything—and that meant she wasn't the only one who needed time. He needed to think about this too. To figure out how much he could tell her, how far he could let her in before she reached the stuff that would just make her kick him out completely. 'This wouldn't...this isn't a fling, Violet, not for me. And I don't think it is for you either. So we can take our time.' Even if the restraint it required was physically painful.

He managed a small smile for her, and shifted just a little further back. 'We'll talk soon, yeah? I need to go figure out all my cutest childhood tales and stories of selfless behaviour to win you over with.'

Violet paused with one hand on her handbag and threw him a serious look. 'Those aren't the ones I want to hear, Tom. I want the truth, same as you. It's the only way I can learn to trust you.' She leant over and pressed a kiss to the side of his mouth before grabbing her room key from the table and heading for the lobby.

The truth. Tom stared after her as she disappeared into the elevator, her golden hair flowing behind her.

The truth was the one thing he definitely *couldn't* tell her.

Draining the rest of his drink, Tom grabbed his own room key and prepared to head up. He had a lot of thinking —and writing—to do.

CHAPTER FOURTEEN

VIOLET HAD A horrible feeling that Tom was avoiding her.

They hadn't talked much on the way home from Brighton, mostly because Tom had been passed out in the passenger seat after muttering something about the mini bar, a spring sticking in his back, a broken window and a dripping shower keeping him awake. Violet hadn't slept much better, but since her room had been perfectly comfortable the only excuse she had was her own thoughts.

She did think, as she got back onto the motorway, that if he'd been that uncomfortable he could have always come and slept in her room...

Except she'd made it very clear that was off the cards, at least until she got to know him a little better. She'd been in a relationship before where the guy knew all her innermost thoughts and dreams and it turned out she didn't know him at all, and look how that ended. But while she knew that was a perfectly sensible decision in principle, that hadn't made it any easier to dismiss the thoughts of what might have happened if she'd just let him kiss her again.

In the days since then, he'd been nowhere to be seen. He hadn't even joined them for dinner last night. 'Working hard', her dad had said with a wink. And Violet might have believed it if it wasn't now *Friday* and she'd seen neither hide nor hair of him all week.

Oh, he'd been around, she knew that much. Locked away in the studio with her dad conducting more of the interviews he had, in fairness, travelled thousands of miles to do. She'd even overheard him talking with her mother once or twice—more interviews, she supposed—before she'd stopped listening at doors and got back to what she was supposed to be doing.

At least getting on with the planning for the Benefit Concert had mostly distracted her. With only a week left to go, she was reaching the hectic last few pages of Rose's carefully made lists. Jake Collins had even sent in the signed rider, so she didn't have to follow through on her publicity threats.

Things were good, and dealing with Jake had given her added confidence to get on with her job. She was on top of everything, had spoken with almost everyone involved, or at least their representatives, personally—without a single mention of the words 'sex' and 'tape' in the same sentence. She was making progress.

But, she had to admit, she missed Tom.

'Miss him how, exactly?' Daisy asked when she came over to try on potential wedding outfits the day before Henry Littlewood's wedding. 'I mean, he's right here.'

Violet sighed, and tried not to think that Rose would have understood. Even her twin would probably have struggled with this one, especially since Violet wasn't sure even *she* understood it.

'I guess I'd just got used to having him around.' She grabbed another dress from the pile of maternity eveningwear Daisy had brought with her. 'How about this one?'

Daisy shook her head. 'Lily Taylor wore that one to a gala last month. It's already been photographed, and I don't want to be in any of those "which mum-to-be wore it best?" comparison pieces.'

So why did you bring it? Violet wanted to ask, but didn't. Pregnancy had made Daisy a little touchy.

'And he's still around.' Daisy shifted on the bed, her hand cupped around her growing baby bump. 'He's just a bit busy interviewing Dad and Mum, I suppose. And me.'

'He's interviewed you?' Violet stopped looking through outfits and stared at her sister.

Daisy blinked back blankly. 'Well, yes. He's interviewing all of us, isn't he?'

'Of course. Yeah.' She'd just imagined that he might start with her.

Daisy shifted again to tug on Violet's hand and make her sit on the bed. 'Okay, seriously. What's going on with the two of you? He's coming as your date tomorrow, Mum said the two of you disappeared to Brighton, of all places, last weekend, and now you tell me you haven't seen him all week. I know you'd probably rather tell Rose, but she's not here. So, fess up—what's going on?'

Violet bit her lip. In some ways, it was probably for the best that Rose wasn't there. She'd have sussed out there was something going on by the time Violet and Tom went for that first lunch. As much as she loved her twin, maybe it was better that she didn't have her über-protective identical sister around right now.

And Daisy…Daisy had always been a good listener, when they'd given her something to listen to.

'To be honest, I have no idea.' Violet fell back to lie on the bed, feeling lighter just for saying it. 'He indicated that he has…feelings, I guess. For me.' By kissing her and making her whole world spin.

'And you said?'

'That it was a bad idea.' Which, now, a week later, felt like a fairly epic mistake in its own right.

'Why?' Daisy asked, eyebrows raised in astonishment.

'He's gorgeous, seems nice, Dad adores him, which is always a good sign, and you're obviously a little bit besotted. So what's the problem? He's…oh. He's a reporter.'

Rose would have got there half an hour ago, but in some ways it was more useful to hear the reasons why Violet *should* say yes. Or maybe that was just wishful thinking.

'Actually, for a reporter, he's kind of…un-slimelike.' The admission didn't come easy.

'You really do like him, don't you?'

Violet sighed. Did she? She thought back over the last couple of weeks. Even after their awful first meeting, when really what she'd most wanted to do was strangle him, there'd still been a weird connection when she'd taken his hand. And he truly had been a help with the Benefit Concert. The way he'd spoken to Olivia's manager… He'd stood up for her, been offended on her behalf. And then he'd taken her out for lunch to cheer her up—and interrogate her, of course. Then he'd come all the way to Brighton and stood back and watched her deal with things herself, and knowing he thought she could had given her the confidence she needed to do it.

He understood about not trusting people. And she hoped he'd understood when she'd told him that she needed to know him better to trust *him*. Hoped he realised that just thinking she might eventually be able to trust him was a huge step for her.

Hoped he wasn't actually avoiding her.

'I do,' she admitted. 'I do like him. I just…he's asking all these questions about my life and my family. By the end of this book, he'll be an authority on all things Screaming Lemons and Huntingdon-Cross. I just want to know him as well. Does that make sense?'

'Of course it does!' Daisy stroked a hand down Violet's arm. 'Oh, Vi, I hope he opens up to you. And if he does…

if he gives you what you've asked for…you'll give him a chance, right? I know it's risky—relationships always are—but we all want to see you happy, and if Tom can make you that way…you have to let him try. Okay?'

Violet nodded. Eight years was too long to hide away, anyway. She'd dealt with pop stars, managers, suppliers and even the press covering the concert over the past week. She could deal with one date with a reporter who made her skin tingle. Right?

Saturday morning came almost too fast for Tom. He'd had a plan, a way to convince Violet that he was worth a chance. She wanted to know all about him? Fine. He'd tell her, up to a point. Nobody really needed to know everything about another person, right? She just needed to feel as if she understood where he came from, and that much he could give her.

Except, he realised quickly, he was always better with the written word than the spoken one. So he'd decided to find the time to write it all down, starting in a freezing, leaking hotel room in Brighton and continuing in between interviews and typing up his notes and a rush job on a short article for an editor who'd called and offered him a last minute slot.

Somehow, it wasn't until Saturday morning that he realised that what he'd written was his own obituary.

Tom stared at the words printed in front of him. Perhaps not the most auspicious start to a relationship, but it did give her all the pertinent information. At least all the information he felt able to share. And it was a start, right? A sign that he could give her what she wanted.

And besides, it was too late to change it now.

A quick shower and Tom dressed in his best suit, ran some gunky stuff through his hair to try and make it behave, and hoped he'd be good enough for the Littlewoods. And Violet.

Rick was already in the kitchen pouring the coffee when Tom made it downstairs, and Daisy's husband, Seb, sat at the counter sipping his own mug as he read the paper.

'Ah, our third compatriot,' Rick said, grabbing another mug and filling it to the brim with hot, strong black coffee. Tom took a sip the moment Violet's father handed it over. Somehow, in the last three weeks, he'd actually converted to *liking* his coffee black. 'This, gentlemen, is the part where we wait.'

Tom checked his watch. 'Aren't we supposed to be leaving soon?'

'Theoretically? Yes. But in reality?' Rick shook his head.

'We told them we needed to leave an hour before we actually do,' Seb explained. 'That way, we might actually get out of here on time.'

Taking a seat, Tom tried to imagine Violet taking hours to get ready. For someone who mostly lived in neat jeans and blouses, with her hair clipped back, it seemed unlikely. But, then again, once Sherry got involved...yeah, he could see things taking a while.

Violet, as a bridesmaid, should, by rights, have stayed at the hotel the night before with the rest of the wedding party. But, as she'd pointed out to everyone at dinner earlier in the week, she was only a bridesmaid on the bride's sufferance, so she wouldn't inflict her presence too early. 'There are, like, ten others anyway. No one is going to miss me.' So, instead. she'd arranged to have her hair and make-up done to match everyone else's at the house and would travel down early with the rest of them.

If she ever finished getting ready.

Two cups of coffee later, Violet appeared, dressed in a

pale blue bridesmaid's dress that left her shoulders bare. Her hair had been pinned back from her face and fell in curls at the back, and her wide dark-lashed eyes looked bluer than ever.

'They are coming, honest. Daisy's just changed her mind about which dress to wear. Again.' Violet swished across the room, her skirt floating around her legs, to fetch herself a coffee. Her shoes were silver, Tom realised. And sparkly.

And he was totally staring.

Blinking, he tore his gaze away, just in time to see Rick hide his smirk behind a coffee cup. Fantastic.

'I'll, uh, go see if the cars are here, shall I?' Tom said, heading out to the front of the house before anyone had time to reply. Maybe the fresh air would help clear his head.

Since they weren't expected for another thirty minutes, of course there were no cars. Stepping to one side of the front door, Tom leant against the brick wall.

'Hey.' He opened his eyes and found Violet standing beside him, cup of coffee in hand. 'You okay?'

'I'm fine,' Tom lied. 'No, actually, I'm not. I have something to give to you, and I'm not sure if I should, if it'll help or if it will scare you off for life…'

Violet raised her eyebrows. 'Well, now you have to give it to me. Because the things I'm imagining just *have* to be worse than whatever the reality is.'

Reaching inside his suit pocket, he pulled out the carefully folded sheet of paper.

'Okay, so you said you wanted to know about me. About my life. And so I thought I'd write it down—that's what I've been doing this week, when I wasn't interviewing your family. So…here it is.' He held out the piece of paper and waited for her to take it, half wishing that she wouldn't.

But she did, her wary eyes huge as they met his. Then she unfolded it, looked down and her eyebrows drew down as her brow furrowed.

'This is… Is this your obituary?'

'Kind of.' Tom hunted for a way to explain. 'When I used to work on a local newspaper, one of the things I was in charge of was keeping the obituaries up to date for local celebrities. So that if anything happened, we were ready to run. I have a few on hand for musicians I've written about or interviewed a lot, too, ready for when the time comes. So when I sat down to write about my life…it just kind of came out that way.'

Violet stared at him. 'You really are a journalist all the way to your core, aren't you?'

'Apparently so.' He just wished that wasn't the one thing she didn't want him to be.

'Is the car here yet, darling?' Sherry's voice floated down the stairs and out of the front door. 'We don't want to be late.'

Violet folded the paper again and slipped it into the tiny silver bag she carried. 'I'll read this later,' she promised. 'And then…maybe we can, uh, talk again?'

'I'd like that a lot,' Tom replied. Of course, first they had to get through the Littlewood wedding. Suddenly, he'd never been so unexcited at the prospect of spending a day with the rich and famous.

CHAPTER FIFTEEN

'So, what do we think?' Daisy asked as they finished up their puddings later that evening. 'Better or worse than my wedding?'

'Our wedding,' Seb put in, around a mouthful of chocolate and pistachio torte. Daisy waved a hand dismissively at him.

'Not a patch on yours, Daze,' Violet assured her sister. 'Was it, Tom? Wait, you weren't there, were you?' Maybe that third glass of champagne had been a bad idea. Bubbles always did go straight to her head.

But there'd been so many people, so many knowing glances. And even with Tom on her arm, she'd needed something else between her and all of them.

'I was not, unfortunately.' Tom smiled across the table at Daisy. 'But, delightful as today has been, I can't imagine it being a patch on a wedding organised by Sherry Huntingdon.'

'A safe bet,' Seb murmured.

Leaning back in her chair, Violet tried to spot the waiters coming round with coffee. Maybe that would help her focus on the special day going on around her.

Because all she'd been able to think about so far was the piece of paper folded up in her clutch bag.

She'd tried to concentrate on smiling as she and the

other bridesmaids walked in front of the beautiful bride down the aisle, and on Henry looking handsomely nervous at the front of the church. And she'd tried to listen to the vicar talking about the importance of love and forgiveness and understanding in a marriage. But really her mind had been buzzing with the knowledge that in her lap she held the history of Tom Buckley. His life and times. His secrets.

And she really, really wanted to know them.

But she wanted the time to savour them, too. To absorb and understand them. And she couldn't exactly sit there and read it at the dining table surrounded by her sister and brother-in-law, and three of Henry's cousins and their wives.

The cousins, fortunately, had wandered off towards the free bar before Daisy had started comparing weddings. But that didn't mean she could just get reading. Did it?

Violet glanced up. Daisy, Seb and Tom were deep in conversation and she didn't seem to be required. Mum and Dad were sitting three tables over, chatting with some old friends. It was entirely possible that no one would notice if she disappeared for ten minutes.

'I'm just going to…' She waved a hand vaguely in the direction of the bathrooms as she stood, but no one seemed bothered.

Pausing in the doorway to the main ballroom, where the wedding breakfast had been served, Violet checked to ensure no one was watching her, then headed in the opposite direction from the bathrooms—towards the gardens.

It was easy enough to find a secluded bench, hidden away behind the walls of the rose garden. If anyone stumbled across her, she could just say she needed a little air. After all, the weather was warm and the five hundred guests had made the ballroom a little stifling. No reason for anybody to suspect anything.

Especially not that she was hiding away to read the obituary of a man still very much alive.

She unfolded the piece of paper, wondering if the fact he'd written it told her more about him than even the words contained could. Only a journalist would think of doing such a thing, which was a permanent worry. But, on the other hand, he'd wanted her to have all the facts, the truth, laid out in a way they were only ever told after death.

This was who he was, how he thought he'd be remembered, everything he felt was important to say about his life. All in two pages—which Violet figured was probably a good page longer than hers would have been. Or a page and a half longer if you omitted the sex tape thing in the interests of good taste.

Yeah. No one was ever going to omit that.

With a deep breath, Violet focused on the words. Even with the dispassionate tone an obituary demanded, she could still hear Tom talking to her with every line.

She lived Tom's childhood in New York, his early career, his estrangement from his mother and his pain at her death, his tours with bands and his relationship history, all in his own words. And by the time she reached the end she almost, almost felt as if he was sitting there beside her.

'So, do you have questions?'

Violet jerked her head up at the sound of Tom's voice, blushing when she found him leaning against the garden wall watching her, one eyebrow raised.

'I probably will have, later.' After all, the plain facts weren't the same as actually *knowing* a person, were they? But after the last few weeks, it was really only the facts that she'd been missing. Swallowing hard, Violet got to her feet. 'But there's something else I want to do first.'

He didn't move as she stepped towards him, and she

understood that this was all on her now. This was her decision. And he would wait and let her make it.

She just hoped it wasn't a mistake.

She stopped, close enough that she could almost feel his breath on her face, but still not touching. Violet looked up into his eyes and saw the control there. He was holding back. So she wouldn't.

Bringing one hand up to rest against his chest, she felt the thump of his heart through his shirt and knew she wanted to be close to that beat for as long as he'd let her. Slowly, she rose up onto her tiptoes, enjoying the fact that he was tall enough that she needed to. And then, without breaking eye contact for a moment, Violet kissed him.

It only took a moment before he responded, and Violet let herself relax into the kiss as his arms came up to hold her close. The celebrity wedding melted away, and all she knew was the feel of his body against hers and the taste of him on her lips. This. This was what she needed. Why had she denied herself this for so long?

And how could it be that kissing Tom somehow tasted like trust?

Eventually, though, she had to pull away. Tom's arms kept her pressed against him, even as she dropped down to her normal height, looking up into his moss-green eyes.

'You liked my obituary, then?' he murmured.

Violet shook her head. 'Not one bit. I'd like it to never be written, please. But…I liked knowing you.'

'Is this where I give you some kind of line about getting to know me even better?' Tom asked, one eyebrow raised.

Violet's laugh bubbled up inside her, as if kissing Tom had released all the joy she'd kept buried deep down. 'I think it probably is, yes.'

'In that case, how long do you think we need to stay at this hootenanny?'

'There's five hundred people here,' Violet pointed out. 'What are the chances of them missing just two?'

'Good point.' And with a warm smile spreading across his face, Tom grabbed Violet's hand and they ran for the waiting car.

'Are you asleep?'

It was many hours later, and Violet's voice was barely more than a whisper. He felt it against his bare skin more than heard it.

'Not quite.' He shifted, pulling her closer against his side. Now he finally had her where he'd dreamt of her being, he wasn't willing to put up with even a centimetre between them. 'You okay?'

'Mmm, fine. More than fine. Kind of awesome, actually.' She smiled sleepily up at him, and he felt a puff of pride at the relaxation and satisfaction he saw in her face. She rubbed her cheek against his chest like a contented kitten.

'Told you this was a good idea,' he murmured into her hair.

Violet laughed, low and warm. 'You did. And you were right.'

Too damn right. This was more than a good idea. This was more than he'd dreamt it could be. He'd known from the first that he was attracted to Violet, but had never really expected to do anything about it. Never imagined he'd want to, not this badly.

But then he'd got to know her. Understand her. Even let her in a bit to understand him. And now look at them.

And she thought it was a good idea, at last.

'I'm glad you think so.'

'Plus, with the…last-minute nature of everything, I'm pretty sure you wouldn't have even had time to set up a video camera.'

It was a joke, he knew, but there was still something brittle behind the words. Something not quite healed. It made him want to wrap her up and keep her safe—not an emotion he was used to feeling about the women he dated. And in this case...he had a feeling that Violet had been kept safe for too long already. She'd had enough of being protected—and she was ready to take care of herself for a change.

Tom sank down a little lower in the bed, turning on his side until they were face to face. 'You know I wouldn't do that, don't you? You have to know that.' She might not need him to protect her, but she did need to trust him. To know he would never, never hurt her.

He wasn't that man any more.

'I do. I do.' Violet inched closer and placed another kiss on his lips. 'I'm just still...adjusting to the idea.'

'I can understand that.' Wrapping his arm around her waist, he pulled her against him. 'I just hope you can learn to trust me.'

'I think I already do.' The hope in Violet's eyes meant he just had to kiss her again.

But when they separated, the hope had faded away and left a question there. 'What is it?' he asked.

'I just wondered...in your obituary, you talked about your mum, how you fell out. And I know you said you hadn't made up when she died. But you never said what you argued about. I guess I just don't understand...what could have been that important that you didn't try to reconcile with her?'

Despite the warmth of the bed and Violet's body, a shiver ran through him and his muscles froze.

'Pride,' he whispered. 'What else? Stupid, pointless pride.'

Violet pressed a kiss against his collarbone. 'Tell me.'

Except he couldn't, could he? Because that one fact, that one omission from his obituary, was the one thing she'd never forgive. Still, he had to tell her something, and the trust in her eyes made him want it to be as close to the truth as he could manage.

'When I was just starting out as a reporter, I worked for a…less reputable paper. The sort that my mom felt was beneath me. It was run by a guy who believed that the ends—a good story—justified any means. And he expected his staff to do whatever they needed to, in order to get the copy.' And slowly, the longer he'd stayed.there, the more desensitised he'd become to those methods.

'Mom said I was wasting my talents, that selling my soul for a job wasn't worth it.' He swallowed at the memory of his mother's face, full of righteous fury. 'She told me she'd brought me up better than that, that she didn't want to know a son who could sink to such depths.'

Tom risked a glance at Violet, where she lay silent, her cheek resting against his shoulder. Her eyes were damp and he fought back against the instinct to tell her how much he didn't deserve her pity or her tears.

'What happened next?' she murmured, her hand caressing his arm, a comforting, caring touch.

'I told her she didn't understand journalism, that she'd never get it. That this was what I had to do to build my career. She kicked me out of the house and told me to come back when I'd found my honour again.' He squeezed his eyes shut. 'It didn't take me too long to figure out she was right. But my pride made me stay away too long. I didn't know she was sick, and by the time I found out…it was too late.'

He'd quit the paper long before then, of course, the moment that terrible story broke and he realised what he'd done. But when he'd lost his mother's respect, he'd lost any respect he had for himself too. How could he go back until he'd regained that? And it turned out respect took far longer to earn than to lose.

Violet wrapped her arms tightly around his middle, shifting until she was almost lying on top of him, protecting him from the world. 'I'm so sorry.'

'It was a long time ago.' As if that made a difference to the pain.

'Still. I wish I could make it better.'

Tom curled his body around hers until they were touching skin at as many points as possible. 'Trust me, you are. Just being with you...watching you move past your own history, it helps.'

'Is that all that helps?' Violet raised her head slightly to look at him, and he felt himself warming at the heat in her blue eyes.

'I can think of one or two other things,' he said, and kissed her again.

CHAPTER SIXTEEN

VIOLET STRETCHED OUT against the sheets, listening to Tom's steady breathing beside her. The sun was almost fully up outside; it had to be around six. She'd heard her parents, Daisy and Seb returning hours ago, listened to their giggles and their good-nights. She'd texted Daisy from the car to say that she and Tom were heading home early—she figured she didn't really need to elaborate. Daisy might not be her twin, but she was still her sister. She knew her well enough for this.

What would they all think? Would they be pleased that she was moving on at last, or scared for her because of whom she'd chosen to move on with? Would they understand? And how would it affect the job that Tom was there to do?

'You're thinking too loudly,' Tom murmured, shifting beside her. 'Go back to sleep.'

'I will,' Violet lied. Running her hand down his arm, she listened until Tom's breathing evened out again. He probably wouldn't even remember his strange comment when he woke up.

But he'd remember the rest of the night, she was sure. That, at least, was impossible to forget. She might not be the most experienced of women, but the chemistry between them, the connection she felt when they were skin against skin…Violet had never felt anything like that before.

She stifled a laugh as she remembered Tom's first words to her—about how the frustrated look on her face reminded him of that hideous tape. Maybe Rose had been right when she'd recounted the incident to her. Maybe she really was finally able to laugh about the whole thing.

That had to mean she was moving on. And it was past time.

She glanced across at Tom, one arm thrown above his head as he slept, his dark hair rumpled and his bare chest so tempting. She could just curl back up beside him right now, rest her head on that chest and drift back to sleep until he woke up again for a repeat performance of last night.

The plan had many, many merits.

With one last look and a quiet sigh, Violet slipped out from between the sheets, slowly enough not to wake him. She needed to think, and that was practically impossible while in bed with Tom. The man was just too distracting—even asleep.

Grabbing a pair of leggings and a long T-shirt from a drawer, and, giving silent thanks that they'd made it back to her room, not Tom's, the night before, Violet dressed silently, then crept out of the room. She'd use the bathroom down the hall to freshen up, rather than her own en suite bathroom, then grab some coffee and head to Rose's study. No one was likely to interrupt her there, at least not for a while. After the late night at the wedding, everyone was likely to sleep in, and Tom…well, he was probably a little worn out too.

She couldn't help the smile that spread across her face as she thought about it. One thing she had no doubt about—last night had *definitely* been a good idea.

Now she just had to figure out what happened next.

The study was blissfully cool, quiet and private. Resting her cup of coffee on the corner of the desk, Violet curled up in her desk chair and stared out of the window. There was probably work for the Benefit that she should be doing, but she knew she'd be good for nothing if she didn't sort out last night in her head first.

He'd talked about his mother, and about the dark side of reporting—as if she didn't know it well enough already. But he'd got out, and the guilt he carried from his mother not knowing that before she'd died...Violet knew that was strong enough to keep him honest for ever. Tom would never be the sort of reporter Nick was. He'd told her the truth about everything.

This could have been history repeating itself all over again—but it wasn't. Because Tom wasn't Nick. And, for the first time in a long time, she honestly found herself hopeful and trusting in her future.

The phone on her desk rang, and Violet frowned at it. Who on earth would be calling so early on a Sunday?

'Violet Huntingdon-Cross,' she said, answering it.

'Miss Cross. It's Jake Collins here.' Ah, of course. Only the most offensive manager on her list of acts—who else? Probably looking for a way to get back at her for the rider thing. 'We're in Dublin airport right now, about to fly back across to your own fair green isle for the Benefit Concert.'

Well, that explained the early morning wake-up call. But not why he was actually calling. And wasn't Ireland the fair green isle, anyway? At least he was sounding civil. Almost friendly, in fact. It was enough to make her suspicious.

'Mr Collins,' she said as brightly as she could, 'how can I help you today?'

'It's rather more a case of how we can help you, I think. I appreciate that the news isn't official just yet, but you know how the industry is. There were enough people at that party last night that it really wasn't a surprise.'

What party? The Littlewood wedding? But the only thing that had happened there... Violet bit back a groan. She'd place money on some camera somewhere catching a shot of her and Tom in the garden. But did anyone really care about that? And what on earth did it have to do with Jake Collins, anyway?

'I'm sorry... I don't understand.' And she wasn't sure she wanted him to explain it, either.

'Of course, of course. I totally get that you need to await the official announcement. And, of course, there will need to be the appropriate period of mourning, especially for your family. But no one would want to see the Benefit Concert cancelled, I'm sure. So all I wanted to say was... if your father feels it inappropriate for the Lemons to perform, Olivia would, of course, be more than happy to help out by taking over the headline slot.'

Mourning? Why would they...and what would make them think of cancelling the concert?

'Mr Collins, really—'

'Oh, I know, too soon. Too soon. But it's out there now. I'll call again at a better time and we can talk. So sorry for your loss. Please, pass my condolences on to your parents.'

The line went dead, and Violet stared at it in her hand for a long moment before a truly dreadful thought hit.

Rose and Will.

Violet's heart beat treble time in her chest. She had no idea where they were, what the time was there and she didn't care. Grabbing her mobile with shaking hands, she pressed the speed dial and prayed for Rose to pick up.

'Vi?' Rose's sleepy voice came over the line and Violet's breath burst out of her in relief.

'Oh, thank God. I just had the strangest phone call and

I thought…never mind. You're okay. Everything's okay.
Go back to sleep.'

''Kay. Call you later.'

Violet hung up. Whatever Jake Collins's deal was, he
was obviously mistaken. Everything was fine. Violet's
heart rate started to return to normal and she reached for
her coffee cup.

She only managed one sip before the police banged on
the door.

'What's going on?' Tom asked as he stumbled into the
kitchen, wishing he'd taken the time to go back to his
own room and find something other than yesterday's suit
to wear. But when he'd woken alone in Violet's bed, heard
voices downstairs then spotted the police cars on the driveway…he hadn't really been thinking about his own sar-
torial elegance.

Violet looked across from the coffee maker, her expression tense. There were lines around her eyes he didn't remember from the night before and they looked puffy and
red, as if she was trying really hard not to cry.

Sherry wasn't even trying. How she managed to still
look beautiful with tears streaming down her face, Tom
had no idea. Rick had one arm around her, his other hand
covering his face. Seb held Daisy in the corner, her face
hidden against his chest.

And next to the kitchen table stood two police officers
and a man in a suit—utterly incongruous in the Huntingdon-Cross kitchen.

'I'm sorry, sir,' the suit said, not sounding at all apologetic. 'I'm Detective Inspector Trivet. And you are?'

'Tom Buckley. I'm here interviewing the family.' Except
he'd never felt more like an outsider than at this moment.

'You're press.' The detective's mouth hardened. 'I'm

sorry, but the family has requested no reporters be allowed in at this time.'

Tom's heart sank, a dead weight in his chest. Of course not. Whatever was happening, this was for family only. 'Right. I'll just—'

'No!' Violet said, too loud in the subdued kitchen. 'Tom's a...family friend. Right, Dad?'

Rick looked up just long enough to nod. His craggy face looked ten years older, Tom realised.

'In that case, I'll tell you just what I've told the others,' Trivet said. 'I'm afraid that in the early hours of this morning one of Mr Cross's cars was discovered along the riverbank, halfway between here and London. The man behind the wheel was Jez Whittle.'

The Screaming Lemons' lead guitarist. But, more importantly this morning, Rick's best friend.

'Is he...?' Tom hardly dared ask. The answer was already written on the face of everyone else in the room.

'It appears that he died in the early hours of this morning.'

'From the car crash?' Tom asked, but Violet shook her head.

'Mr Whittle died from a fatal overdose of heroin.' Trivet's expression was solemn as he spoke. 'People at the party he'd attended in London confirmed that he had seemed unstable before he left and had talked about needing "something more" to take the edge off.'

'He'd been clean for years!' Rick's head shot up, his distress clear on his face. 'I mean, twenty years. You don't just fall off the wagon after two decades. Not without talking to someone first. Without talking to *me*.'

Oh, God, he shouldn't be here. This wasn't meant for Tom to witness. He shouldn't be watching Violet go to her parents and wrap her arms around them both, tears on her cheeks. Because if he was here…he had to write about this moment. Had to tell this story.

And how could he, now?

'What happens next?' Seb asked, his voice low and even. He was family now, even if he'd only married in. He could take charge and ask questions and take care of people. While Tom had to just fade into the background and pretend he wasn't intruding on this incredibly private grief.

Except he wanted to. He wanted to take Violet in his arms the way Seb had held Daisy, wanted to make this easier for her, any way he could.

'There'll be an official inquest, of course,' the detective said. 'And we'll need to ask Mr Cross a few questions about the car and such. But mostly, I imagine, you can expect an influx of paparazzi, and soon. I can leave a couple of uniforms here to watch the door, if you want. Might dissuade most of them from trying anything extreme.'

Like climbing in through windows, harassing the family every time they even looked outside. Oh, God, this was going to be hell for Violet.

Seb nodded. 'Thank you. And if that's all…' The Earl had the aristocracy's way with dismissal hints, Tom realised, and almost smiled.

'For now.' Detective Inspector Trivet motioned towards the door with his head and the policemen all filed out, leaving the family alone. With Tom.

'I should…' Leave, he wanted to say. But how could he when Violet's head jerked up, her blue eyes huge and wide in her pale face and her gaze pleading. 'Make more coffee,' he finished. 'Or food. If anyone wants something to… Or something else. Anything you need.'

'Thank you,' Violet whispered. But no one else was listening.

'I don't *understand* it.' Rick crashed his fist down onto

the table, rattling the coffee cups. 'Why didn't he talk to me? Of all the people...he knew! He knew I could help.'

'I set up a drug rehab and addiction counselling centre years ago.' Rick's words from one of many interviews floated through Tom's mind. *'I always felt it was important to pay back, for all the narrow escapes friends have had. I wanted to help.'*

And was this why? Had Rick been thinking about Jez when he'd started that project? That it would have made his friend's life easier—or even that it would be there, ready for him, if he ever needed it again?

Stories of Jez's addictions had appeared in the papers regularly, back in the day. But the band had always closed ranks around him, Tom remembered from his research. And in those days they hadn't had the internet or camera phones to contend with. By the time they'd been invented, Jez had sobered up and flown right.

Until last night.

'He was probably on his way here, Rick.' Sherry sounded exhausted, even though they'd all only been up for an hour or so, Tom guessed. 'He always, always came here when he was in trouble, you know that. He came to us and we fixed it.'

'Except this time he left it too late.' Rick's melancholy tone tore another sob from Daisy, and Violet looked paler than ever. Her hands were shaking, Tom realised. He wanted to go to her. Wanted to know what to say, how to help.

But then the phone rang and Tom realised there was, at least, one thing he could do.

'That'll be the papers,' Sherry said softly.

'Vultures.' Rick glanced up. 'No offence, Tom.'

'None taken,' Tom assured him.

'Do we answer it?' Daisy asked. 'Or just leave it.'

'They won't stop calling,' Seb said.

Tom took a breath. It wasn't his place. He wasn't part of the family.

But he would do this for Violet.

'I'll deal with them,' he said. 'All of them. You just… look after each other, and don't worry about the press, or the photographers, any of it. I'll take care of it all.'

He wasn't quite sure if Violet's expression was grateful or concerned, but it didn't matter. If she didn't trust him completely after this, she never would.

CHAPTER SEVENTEEN

NOTHING WAS EVER going to be the same again.

It wasn't the first time Violet had experienced that sort of revelation in her life, but this time it felt impossible to see how her family would ever find their way back to being whole again. The grief they were all experiencing permeated the house, a silence that crept through the hallways and clung to the curtains.

That silence had sent her running for Rose's study, the place she'd spent the most time over the last few weeks. The place she'd hoped would help her take control of her life again, to grow up and start living instead of just hiding.

But hiding was all she wanted to do now.

Uncle Jez. She'd known him since before she was born, had grown up with him always there for birthdays and parties and jam sessions and just when he was craving ice cream. He had free run of the house—especially the kitchen if he felt like making pancakes. He'd treated Dad's collection of cars as his own, had famously said he could never marry because Rick had stolen the only woman worth settling down for, then gone on and married—and divorced—four times. He was wild and free and enormous fun and she would miss him, always, in a corner of her heart that would never heal.

But most of her grief was for her parents. For their loss.

And for the horrible, unexpected proof that everything they'd told her, her whole life, was wrong.

Everything wouldn't be okay if they just stuck together. As long as they had each other, terrible things could still happen. There were some things in this world that family just couldn't fix.

And the worst thing was that she'd known that, really, of course she had. But she'd never actually believed it until this morning.

'Hey.' Tom stuck his head around the door at the same time as he rapped his knuckles lightly across the wood. 'Do you need anything?'

He hadn't asked if she was okay, which she appreciated. In fact, he'd been great at avoiding the stupid, unnecessary comments and questions and just getting on with what needed to be done. He'd gone out and faced the pack of press hyenas outside the house and asked that they respect the family's privacy and grief at this terrible time—not that any of them imagined that they would. Still, it had made it clear that no one intended to make a fool of themselves in front of them, or give them a new sound bite or photo to focus on.

Violet had watched him on the telly, too scared to even risk appearing at a window hiding behind a curtain to see it live. He'd looked in control, but also as if he cared.

As if he was part of the family.

Violet took a breath. 'To be honest, I could do with a hug.'

'That, I can do.' Tom smiled and shut the door behind him. Stepping forward, he opened up his arms and she practically jumped into them. How had it only been a matter of hours since she'd been curled up naked in his arms? And how could so much have changed since then?

'Rose is on her way back,' she murmured after a long

moment of just being held. 'At least she hopes so. She and Will were heading to the airport to see if they could get an earlier flight home when I spoke to them last. Although, since I still have no idea where they are, God only knows how long it will take them. I said I'd go pick them up if they let me know when their flight gets in.'

'I'll come with you,' Tom said. 'Just let me know when.'

'I'd like that.' Violet wondered if he could sense the relief in her voice. She could have sent a car, but it was important to her that Rose saw family when she arrived. But that didn't mean she wouldn't appreciate some backup when the inevitable comments and photos and looks started at the airport.

Strange to think that this time they'd be because of Uncle Jez rather than her own mistakes.

'How's your dad doing?' Tom asked and Violet pulled back from his arms with a sigh. Back to the real world.

'He's…devastated, basically. Mum's with him, though, so that will help. Daisy and Seb are going to stay on for the next week, too. Seb's popped home to get their stuff, and Daisy has gone for a lie down.'

'And you? How are you doing?' That question at last. She supposed even Tom couldn't hold off asking it for ever.

'I'm…angry. At Uncle Jez, at those vultures outside our door—no offence—at the world.' But Violet had learned that just being angry didn't get you anywhere. You had to do something with it or it was just wasted.

She'd spent the last eight years being pointlessly angry, and look where it had got her.

'I realised I'm angry because it's so meaningless,' she said, looking straight into Tom's eyes. 'So I decided to make it mean something.'

Tom blinked. 'Mean something. How, exactly?'

Taking a deep breath, Violet held up the new poster

mock-up she'd spent the morning working on. 'I know the concert's only five days away, and I know this would mean a ridiculous amount of work to pull it off—especially since we don't even know if Dad and the rest of the boys will even want to get on stage. But what do you think? Will you help me?' Violet glanced down at her newly appropriated poster, now proclaiming the Benefit Concert to be wholly in support of addiction support centres across the country. It would be a lot to do. But it would definitely mean something. It would be worth it.

A smile spread across Tom's face, and she knew she had him.

'Just tell me what you need me to do,' he said.

Violet had spent two days working like a woman possessed. Tom watched her in awe, taking every task she gave him and completing it as efficiently as possible, mostly because he wanted to get back to watching her work. If he'd ever thought of her as a spoilt celebrity kid who only wanted the spotlight without having to do anything beyond getting naked to earn it—and, okay, he had—she was proving him wrong by the second.

She amazed him. All day long she made the calls he knew would have terrified her a few weeks ago, speaking to not just people in the business but the media too. She fended off questions about her family and her dad's reaction to Jez's death like a pro, as though they didn't touch her at all. Tom knew they did—knew that when she clung to him in their bed at night she was thinking of all those people out there, desperate to know every detail of her life and use it against her.

He did his best to distract her at those moments.

And she amazed him there, too. When she wasn't being professional Violet, organising the Benefit almost from the ground up again, or family Violet, taking care of her distraught parents and pregnant sister, or even community Violet, fending off well-meaning locals who came with flowers or food. When she could just be his Violet, alone in the dark, letting him see the heart of her. As if Jez's death had torn down the last of her barriers and given him a clear path in to the real Violet.

They'd never really had The Talk—the one about their future and what they both expected out of this relationship, if it even was a relationship. But somehow, Tom felt, they didn't need to. They'd instinctively moved past that, to an understanding that this was what it was—and it was what they both needed right now. They mattered to each other, and the world was easier with each other in it. That was all Tom cared about.

'Okay, so what's left?' Violet asked, tapping her pen against her notepad as she frowned down at her list.

Tom refrained from pointing out that she was the one with the checklist in front of her. Instead, he moved behind her, rubbing her shoulders firmly as he looked down at the lines after lines of her handwriting, all with tiny check boxes beside them.

'Well, most of the stuff that needed printing—the new signs and programmes and stuff—that's all taken care of,' he said, assessing the ticks in the check boxes. 'And we've spoken to every act and sponsor and media partner between us, so they all know the score.'

'And they're all on board,' Violet added, a hint of amazement in her voice. As if she couldn't believe that *she'd* actually talked them all into it.

'With your incredible persuasive sell? Of course they are.' Tom dug his fingers into a particularly tight knot in her back. 'The riders for all the acts are sorted—even Olivia's. And all the technical stuff is more or less unchanged.

The new wristbands and such are en route, ready to hand out to the vendors when they arrive, to sell alongside everything else. What else is there?'

Violet's shoulders stiffened, beyond the power of his fingers to relax them. 'The headline act.'

'Apart from that.' Tom let out a long breath and moved his hands to just rest against Violet's skin, a reminder that he was there, that he wanted to help. 'Have you spoken to your dad yet?'

'Not about this,' Violet said. 'About the funeral arrangements, about the good old days, about the clinic, about what he'd have done to help if Jez had just come to him… But not a word on if The Screaming Lemons are planning to perform at the Benefit Concert.'

'He hasn't spoken to any of the rest of the band either,' Tom confirmed. 'Jonny actually asked *me* yesterday if I knew what was going on.'

'I need to ask him.' Violet put down her pen, obviously not willing to add this action to the list. 'If he wants to play…we need to get in another guitarist. They've worked with some great session musicians over the years…'

'Actually,' Tom said, the word out before he'd even completed the thought, let alone decided if it was a good idea, 'I might know someone. Someone I think your dad would approve of.'

Violet turned in her seat, twisting under his hands until she was almost in his arms. 'Really? Who?'

Tom shook his head. He didn't want to get her hopes up if it didn't work out. 'Look, you talk to your dad first. If he says he wants to go on…I'll make some calls.'

'Okay.' She gave him the sad half smile he'd grown too used to seeing over the past few days. 'Thank you, Tom. For everything you've done this week. I know this wasn't exactly what you came to Huntingdon Hall for.'

'Neither was this.' He dipped his head to press a kiss against her lips. 'And I wouldn't give us up for the world.'

A faint pink blush spread across her cheeks. Was that a step too far? Too close to the 'talking about things' line they weren't crossing? Because if there was one thing Tom had realised over the last couple of days, it was that he *wanted* to talk about things between them. He wanted to put a name on their relationship.

He wanted to tell her he had fallen in love with her.

But now wasn't the time. After the Benefit, once things had calmed down, and once Rose was back and her family was a little more stable again. They had time. He just had to pick the right one.

Love, it turned out, was worth waiting for.

'I mean it, Tom.' Violet's expression turned serious. 'You came here for a tell-all book, the exclusive stories that would make your name. And here you are, in the middle of the biggest story to hit the Lemons in thirty years, and you're spending all your time telling other reporters "no comment". I know it can't be easy for you—you're a born journalist; we both know that. But you haven't chased this story, haven't exposed Dad's grief. And I really, really appreciate that.'

Tom's smile felt fake and forced. A born journalist. Was that what he'd always be to her? And, worse, was it true? 'Of course I wouldn't. I'm here for you right now—and not as a reporter. When your dad is ready to resume our interviews, fine. But for now…let's just focus on the Benefit, yeah?'

Violet nodded. 'Are you still coming with me to the airport to fetch Rose and Will this afternoon?' The honeymooning pair had ended up having to take three separate flights over thirty-six hours to get home just one day earlier than planned, but Rose had insisted on doing it anyway.

'I'll be there,' Tom promised. 'I'll meet you at the front door at two, yeah?'

'Okay.' Violet leant up and pressed a kiss to his mouth. 'And, in the meantime, I need to go talk to Dad.'

'You do.' Neither of them were admitting it, but if the Lemons didn't play at the concert, the Benefit would lose a lot of impact. Yes, people might understand Rick's reluctance to get back on stage so soon after Jez's death, might even respect it. But without Rick Cross on stage, the Huntingdon Hall Benefit would just be another concert. And Violet, Tom knew, wanted this year's Benefit to be much, much more than that. She wanted to use it to change attitudes, to promote the availability of aid—for addicts and their friends and family.

She wanted to make a difference, and Tom honestly believed she might.

Plus, if there was anyone who could talk Rick Cross into anything, it had to be Violet.

'Wish me luck,' Violet said.

'You don't need it,' Tom told her, but he kissed her again for luck anyway. Just in case.

CHAPTER EIGHTEEN

VIOLET JANGLED THE car keys in her hand, barely resisting the urge to tap her foot. Where was he? It was quarter past two and still no sign of Tom. She really had to leave to fetch Rose and Will—unless she wanted them grumpy and fed up after a thirty-six hour flight with no one there to meet them.

'Any sign?' Sherry appeared through the kitchen door.

Violet shook her head. 'You haven't seen him either?'

'Afraid not. I checked the study again, and his room.'

'Did you ask Dad?' Violet asked, then regretted it when Sherry's face turned a little grey. Rick hadn't been in the best mood after Violet's conversation with him that afternoon.

'He's shut himself away in the studio,' Sherry said. 'I thought it best to leave him for now.'

'Yeah, I can understand that.' Guilt knotted in her gut. She shouldn't have pushed him, certainly not so soon. It was just that she was so desperate to make this year's Benefit Concert more of a success than ever. For Uncle Jez.

'Violet…' Her mother paused, and Violet felt the knot in her stomach twist tighter.

'I know what you're going to say, Mum. Don't worry. I'm not going to pester him again.'

But Sherry shook her head. 'It's not that. Sweetheart…

we're so proud of how you've stepped up these past few weeks. Taking over the Benefit, dealing with everything— even Tom being here.' She gave Violet a sly smile. 'Although I suspect that one wasn't quite the hardship you imagined, right?'

'Mum, I—'

'Darling, I think it's marvellous. He's a great guy, and it was past time for you to find something worth coming out of hiding for. No, all I wanted to say was…I'm so proud of what you're doing, turning this Benefit into a fitting memorial for your Uncle Jez, and a way to help others who might not know where to turn. It's important work, and I know how much it took for you to do it.'

Violet's eyes burned. 'Thanks, Mum.'

'So, so proud, darling.' Sherry wrapped her arms around her daughter and squeezed her lightly in a hug. 'And I do think the Lemons should play. I know your father isn't quite there yet, but I think he will be, once some of the fog clears. So…I'll talk to the boys, get them all on board. So we're ready when your dad bursts out of that studio ready to take to the stage, yes?'

'That would be great. Thanks, Mum.' Violet hugged her back, thinking, not for the first time, that the whole family would have been doomed years ago if Sherry hadn't been there to take them in hand.

'Now, you get off and fetch that twin of yours and her husband. We need all the family here right now.' She made a shooing motion with her hands. 'Go on. I'll tell Tom you couldn't wait for him when he shows up. He's probably on a call or something.'

Sherry was probably right, Violet decided as she pulled out of the garage and prepared to drive past the reporters still camped out on their doorstep. Tom wouldn't have left her to do this alone unless something important had come up. And since he'd taken on the job of distracting and dealing with the media and their many, many questions about Uncle Jez and the family, the chances were he was probably yelling 'no comment' down the phone at someone he'd previously considered a friend and colleague right now.

'Violet! Violet!' The calls started the moment her car pulled around to the front of the house and headed for the driveway out to the main road. She checked her windows were completely shut, but it didn't seem to do much for keeping the shouts out.

'How's your dad?' someone called.

'Any news on the car? How did Jez get hold of it?' yelled a less concerned reporter.

'Are Rose and Will coming home?'

'Is it true that Daisy went into premature labour and is now on bed rest?'

Violet had to smile at that one. Daisy was only five months pregnant and, if she was in bed, Violet was pretty sure she was 'seeking solace' in the arms of her rather attractive husband. Really, did they not think if something had happened to the baby they'd have seen the ambulances and medical experts lined up by the dozen? Sherry Huntingdon was taking absolutely no chances with her first grandchild.

The questions followed her as she sped down the driveway and faded away as she hit the open road. It was strange to think that the last time she'd driven this way had been when she'd headed to the airport to collect Tom. So much had changed since then, she barely recognised the frustrated, lonely woman who'd let loose on him in the coffee shop.

In the end, it turned out that Rose and Will's last leg flight had been delayed. Sighing as she checked the arrivals board for updates, Violet spotted a familiar-looking coffee shop and decided that was as good a place as any to try and avoid attention. Picking up a paper on her way, she grabbed a coffee, settled herself into a corner where she could still see the screens with flight information and prepared to wait.

She heard a few murmurs as people spotted her, probably exacerbated by the fact that the front page of the newspaper had a splashy sidebar about Jez's autopsy, but no one approached her directly, which Violet appreciated. In fact, it was possibly the most peace and quiet she'd had in days.

She should have known it wouldn't last.

Violet was halfway through reading an editorial piece about the price of fame, idly making her own comments in the margins with a pencil, when her phone rang. She didn't recognise the number, but that wasn't exactly unusual these days. She had all the main contacts for the Benefit Concert programmed in, but every time someone rang from a different office line or their home phone instead of their mobile, it threw her off.

'Violet Huntingdon-Cross,' she answered, trying to sound both welcoming—in case it was someone from the Benefit—and dismissive—in case it was another reporter who'd got hold of her number—at the same time.

'Hello, sweetpea.' The voice on the other end made her muscles freeze up, her whole body tense. For eight years she'd avoided that voice, and the man it belonged to. Eight years she'd spent trying to pretend he didn't exist—which was almost true. The man she'd thought she loved didn't exist at all. Only this man, who could betray her in a moment for a good story.

'Nick.' She should hang up, switch her phone off and pretend this never happened. Go back to hiding away from him and everything he represented.

Except she wasn't that Violet any more, was she?

'What do you want?' she asked, her tone clipped. She was so far past him now. One little conversation wouldn't kill her.

'The same thing everything wants from you right now,' Nick said. 'An official comment on the recent untimely death of your father's lead guitarist.'

Violet laughed, loud enough to draw attention from the people sitting at the next table. 'Why on earth would you imagine I'd give you that?' Or anything else he wanted, for that matter.

'Maybe for old times' sake?' Nick said. 'But I suppose I should have known better.'

'Too right you should.'

'I mean, you've got another journo on the line these days, haven't you? Stringing you along, just waiting for the story of a lifetime. I bet old Tom couldn't believe his luck.'

'You know Tom?' It wasn't really a question; Nick had always known everyone. Tom might be from the other side of the pond, but that wouldn't mean much. They ran in the same circles. But Nick was wrong if he thought Tom was anything like him.

'Doesn't everybody?' Nick said lightly. 'But I suppose the real question is how well *you* know Tom. I mean, have you ever read through his stories? Not the recent ones, but the early stories. The story that gave him his first big break, for example.'

'I don't know what you're talking about, and I don't want to.' Violet swallowed down the fear that rose up her throat as she remembered Tom talking about the first paper he'd worked for. The one that had caused such a rift between him and his mother. He'd never talked about the stories he wrote for that paper…a fact she'd wilfully ignored in the face of their romance. 'Tom's not like you. And what the hell does it matter to you anyway?'

'Maybe I just couldn't bear to see you taken in so completely all over again.' There was a pause, then Nick laughed. 'Okay, take this call as your reminder. When you figure out what he's really like and you realise that we're all the same, us journos, perhaps you might think *better the devil you know*, yeah? You've got to talk some time. Might as well talk to me as the next man.'

'It will never be you,' Violet bit out. How could he even think that? And what did he think he knew about Tom that would make *Nick* seem like the better option? She couldn't even think about it. 'Goodbye, Nick.'

She ended the call, her heart still racing. He was probably just winding her up. Taking a chance on having an in on the story of the century, or whatever. His editor had probably put him up to it. He couldn't have ever imagined she'd actually talk to him, right?

Which meant he was probably making it up about Tom, too. What the hell did Nick know, anyway? All Tom's stories were music based—even his early ones for that cursed paper were probably album reviews. What could possibly be contentious in that? Maybe he gave the Lemons two stars once or something, but that wasn't enough to drive a wedge between them. The past was the past; it didn't matter now.

Except…Nick had said they were all the same. And Violet knew some of the stories Nick had written. Had starred in a few.

Tom wouldn't write anything like that. Would he?

Violet glanced up at the arrivals screen. Still no word. So she had time to kill. It didn't mean anything.

At least that was what she told herself as she pulled her tablet out of her bag and began a search on Tom's name.

It took less time than she'd imagined. She wasn't exactly an internet geek, but even she could find basic information on a person—and the articles they'd written. And it wasn't exactly hard to figure out which one Nick had been referring to.

There, in amongst all the album reviews, band interviews and concert coverage, dated ten years earlier, was the story that had started Tom Buckley's career. And it made Violet's stomach turn just to read it.

Teenage starlet in nude photo scandal.

The photos had clearly been taken up close and in person, rather than by telephoto lens. Whoever had taken them had got close. Very close. And had been invited there.

Violet remembered the story breaking, remembered how these very photos had been splashed across the news, the papers and the internet within a matter of hours. And the text, the background info…he'd gone out looking for this, Violet could tell. Maybe he'd had a tip-off, maybe he'd played a hunch—whatever. Tom had deliberately and wilfully pursued and exposed this story. And maybe even seduced the actress to do it.

Kristy Callahan had been barely eighteen at the time, Violet remembered. She'd been famous for starring in a wholesome family sitcom. And Tom's story had destroyed her career.

Violet didn't want to know this. But now that she did… she couldn't pretend the story didn't exist. That she didn't know what Tom had done. He hadn't fallen out with his mother over the paper he worked for—it was because of this story. It had to be. He'd been lying to her after all, just at the moment she'd thought she had the truth. That she could trust him.

She glanced up at the screen; Rose and Will's plane had landed at last. She needed to find her sister and her best friend.

And then she needed to go home and find Tom.

CHAPTER NINETEEN

GOD, WHAT A DAY. Tom had been surprised when Rick had called him into his studio, and stunned when he'd insisted on doing an interview right now.

But the material he'd got was golden.

'I think, whenever you lose someone close to you, you always wonder if there was something more you could have done. Some small thing that would have kept them with you.' Rick shook his head, staring down at his hands. 'With Jez…knowing that I really *could* have done more—that I could have saved him if he'd let me, if he'd just called. That's going to be hard to live with. As is the guilt. Wondering if I should have seen the signs sooner, should have taken more precautions.'

Tom swallowed before asking his next question, reminding himself that today Rick was a subject, not a friend, not the father of the woman he was in love with. That he was here to do a job—one Rick had hired him for. That meant not shying away from the hard questions.

'Do you think…were there signs? Ones that you missed?'

Rick sighed. 'Probably. But, then again, maybe not. When an addiction takes hold…sometimes it can be a slow build towards cracking again, but more often it can just be one moment, one instant that flips you from recovering to addict again. There's such a thin line…and sometimes Jez liked to walk it. To put himself in the way of temptation.' He shook his head again. 'I don't know. If he wanted to hide it from me, he knew how. And with everything that's been going on here the last few months…maybe I wasn't paying the attention that I should have been.'

Guilt was etched in Rick's craggy face, whatever his words. Tom knew that guilt. That was the sort that never went away, the type you could never make up for once that moment had passed, the opportunity had been missed.

Rick Cross would blame himself for his best friend's death for the rest of his life, whether there was anything he could have done to prevent it or not. Facts didn't matter here, only love.

'Dad?' The door to the studio creaked open and Violet appeared through it. 'Rose and Will are here. And…have you seen…?' She trailed off as she caught sight of him. Tom gave her an apologetic smile, hoping she wasn't too mad about him missing the airport run. He'd planned to talk to her about it, but Rick had been very insistent that the interview was happening now or not at all.

'They're here?' Rick wiped his cheeks with the back of his hands and jumped to his feet. 'Sorry, Tom. We'll do this later, yeah?'

But Violet wasn't looking at her dad. She was still staring at Tom. And he had a horrible feeling that this might just have been his last interview with Rick Cross.

'I'm sorry I couldn't come to the airport with you,' Tom said as Rick shut the door behind him. 'Was it okay?'

'What were you talking to Dad about just then?' Violet's tone was clipped and her gaze sharp. 'Never mind; I'd rather hear it anyway.' She held out a hand for his phone and, with a sense of foreboding, Tom handed it over.

'He asked me to come in here,' he said as she fiddled

with the settings. 'He wanted to talk about some things with me now, while they were still fresh. He said you'd asked him about going on stage for the concert and he wasn't sure. He still needed to work some things out. He thought doing the interview might help.'

He sounded as if he was making excuses, Tom knew, when he had nothing to excuse. He'd been doing his job—and trying to help Rick at the same time. And Violet, for that matter, if it helped him get back on stage for the Benefit.

She had absolutely no reason to be mad at him, and yet he was pretty damn sure she was.

Violet pressed play and Rick's voice filled the room, cracked and broken and distraught.

'I think, whenever you lose someone close to you, you always wonder if there was something more you could have done. Some small thing that would have kept them with you. With Jez...knowing that I really could have done more—that I could have saved him, if he'd let me, if he'd just called. That's going to be hard to live with. As is the guilt. Wondering if I should have seen the signs sooner, should have taken more precautions.'

Violet jabbed a finger at the phone and the voice stopped.

'This is why you came, isn't it?' she said, her voice too even, too calm. 'I think I forgot that, with...everything that happened between us. But you were only ever here to do a job, weren't you? To find out all the dirty little secrets in the closets of my family and friends and put them on display for the world to see. Uncle Jez said—' She broke off, and Tom could see her hands trembling as she held his phone. He wanted to go to her so much it burned. 'He told my dad to find a better closet to hide those skeletons in. But in the end, he was the biggest story you could have hoped for, wasn't he? You must have been so frustrated to miss all the drama of Daisy's wedding, and then Rose's too. But at least there was still one sister here for you to get close to and seduce. And then Uncle Jez overdosed in Dad's car and you realised you had the story of the century right here. An interview with a grief-stricken Rick Cross. All you had to do was make sure none of the other journalists got to him first.' She gulped back a sob, and the sound broke his heart. 'And to think I thought you were doing *us* a favour, turning them all away.'

'Violet, no. You're wrong.' She had to be wrong. None of this had been planned—least of all the part where he fell for her. 'I told you. I'm not that kind of journalist.' He just had to reason with her. She was upset, and that was understandable, but she'd come round once she calmed down and saw the truth. That was all. He just had to be patient and not lose his temper and everything would be fine. 'Your dad asked me to come here; you know that. And he asked for the interview today.' He stepped closer, reaching out for her, but she flinched away. 'And I know you've had bad experiences before so I understand why you might be a bit sensitive—'

'A bit *sensitive?'*

Tom winced. 'Bad choice of words. I mean, I can see why you might worry about these things. But you don't need to. I'm not like your ex. I'm one of the good guys.'

'Yeah?' Violet's expression tightened. 'And is that what you told Kristy Callahan?'

The bottom dropped out of Tom's lungs, leaving him fighting to suck in the air he needed to respond. Just the sound of her name sent the guilt crashing in waves over his shoulders and, in that moment, he knew just how Rick felt. Worse, because Rick hadn't actually done anything wrong. Whereas he had known exactly what he was doing and had done it anyway.

God, Violet was right. He was every bit as bad as her ex; he just hid it better.

'How did you…? Never mind.' It didn't matter now, anyway. She knew, and that was enough. 'I can explain. Will you listen to me?'

Violet barked a laugh, harsh and uncompromising. 'Listen to you? I don't even need to, Tom. I know exactly what you're going to say. That she knew what she was doing. She was a celebrity; she knew the score, and the risks. That it was different then—that she meant nothing to you. That *I'm* different…we're different. If you're really desperate, you'll probably trot out the love line. How being with me has changed you, that now you love me you could never do something like that again.'

The vitriol and bitterness in her words was sharp enough to cut, and the worst part was that she was right. He'd tell her anything to win her back right now. And she'd never believe it was because he truly did love her.

She'd never believe anything he ever said again.

But he still had to try.

'It was a mistake. I was just starting out and the paper I worked for… I didn't take those photos; you have to believe that much. I wouldn't do that.'

'No, you'd just syndicate them in papers and news outlets around the world.' Her mouth tightened again. 'This was the real reason you fell out with your mother, isn't it? This was what she couldn't forgive.'

'Yes. It was. But…it wasn't like you think.' He had to find some way to make her understand. She might never trust him again, and his chances of getting her to fall in love with him were non-existent now. He'd thought he had time, and now he was scrambling just to make her believe he wasn't the biggest scumbag on the planet.

Which, given some of his past actions, was a lot harder than he'd like.

'Really, Tom? You're going to try and tell me what it was like?' She gave him a mocking half smile. 'Trust me, I know. I lived it, after all.'

No. He wouldn't let her think that he was just like her ex. He'd made a mistake, sure, but he hadn't planned it. Hadn't deliberately set out to destroy that girl. And she had to know that.

'It's not the same. Violet, you have to listen to me—'

'No! I don't! Not any more. I listened to you, right from that first night. And I should have known better. I *knew* what you were, and I *knew* how this would end. I should never have let you in, never let you close.' She shook her head sadly. 'You said it the night we met. I was never anything more than the Sex Tape Twin to you. Someone you could use to get what you wanted because I didn't matter at all. I'm just a punchline, right? Just a grainy video on the internet for late night comedians to use to get a cheap laugh, even all these years later.'

How could she think that? After everything they'd shared, after the way they'd been together?

'You know the worst part?' Violet asked. 'I actually trusted you. All that talk about never trusting anyone outside my family and I just let you in. Because you were nice to me.' She laughed, low and bitter. 'How desperate must I have been? God, you must have thought you had it made.'

Anger rolled through his body, working its way up through his chest and finding its way out of his mouth before he could even think to censor his words.

'You talk about trust? If you trusted me one iota you'd listen to me. You'd let me explain. You'd trust me enough not to jump to the worst conclusion at the first sign of trouble.' Violet stepped back at the force of his words, and he wanted to feel bad about that but he couldn't find it in himself. 'How did you even find out about that story? Did you go hunting for a reason to put between us? Or did someone tip you off?' The faint splash of pink that coloured her cheeks told him that he'd hit the mark. 'Who was it? Rose? Or another reporter?' The obvious truth slammed into him and he almost laughed at the ridiculousness of it. 'It was him, wasn't it? After everything he did to you, you still trust his word over mine.'

'I trust facts!' Violet shot back. 'How I found out doesn't matter—except that it wasn't from you. If you want my trust, you have to give me the truth.'

'How could I tell you this?' Tom asked. 'Violet, you've been hiding away here so long, so scared of what people might think or say, you don't even know what trust looks like any more. You wouldn't even talk to me about whether we were in a relationship! I was falling madly in love with you and I couldn't even say the words in case I spooked you. In case you jumped to exactly the conclusions you ran to today.'

'The *right* conclusions,' Violet countered, conveniently ignoring all his other points.

'No.' The anger faded, as fast as it had come, and all Tom was left with was that cold, hard certainty. 'You're wrong about me. I made a mistake ten years ago. But since I've come here the only mistake I've made was believing that you could move past *your* mistakes, your history, and find a future with me.'

Violet stared at him, her eyes wide, and for just a moment he thought she might actually listen to his side of the story. Then she held out his phone and her thumb grazed the play button again.

'*Do you think...were there signs? Ones that you missed?*'

His own voice, pressing Rick for more answers, a deeper admission of guilt.

Violet's face turned stony at the sound.

Rick's heavy sigh echoed around the studio.

'*Probably. But then again, maybe not. When an addiction takes hold...sometimes it can be a slow build towards cracking again, but more often it can just be one moment, one instant that flips you from recovery to addict again. There's such a thin line...and sometimes Jez liked to walk it. To put himself in the way of temptation.*'

She pressed 'stop' again and dropped the phone to the table as if it were poisoned.

'I'm not ignoring the signs,' she said, each word like a bullet. 'And I'm not staying anywhere near temptation. I want you to leave. Today.'

'Your father—' He couldn't go. Never mind the story of a lifetime; if he left her now Tom knew Violet would never let him back in, no matter how fast he talked.

'Will understand when I explain exactly what you've done.' Her eyes were cold, her arms folded across her chest like a shield. 'You're just a reporter. I'm family. Trust me on this. I know which one he's going to choose.'

So did Tom. And he knew when he was beaten.

He gave a slight nod and reached for his phone. 'I'll pack now and be gone within the hour.'

He'd gambled everything on this being more than a story. Time to admit he'd lost.

'Goodbye, Violet.'

CHAPTER TWENTY

VIOLET STOOD SHAKING in the middle of the studio for long minutes after Tom left. She needed to move, needed to talk to Rose, needed to explain to her father what she'd done. But how could she when she felt as if her heart, along with some other essential internal organs, had been ripped out?

She'd known, from the moment she saw that story with his name on it, exactly how the day would go. Had known she'd be standing here alone again at the end of it. Seeing Tom abuse her father's trust and exploit his grief for a story had only made it easier.

She'd made the right decision. She'd got out before Tom could tear her life apart again.

So why did she feel so broken all the same?

'Violet, honey?' When had her dad come in? How had she missed that? 'Where's Tom? Your mum said she just saw him walking out the front with a suitcase.'

'I told him to leave.' The words came out as barely more than a whisper. Would Dad be mad? He'd invited Tom here, after all. He was his guest—his employee, really. It hadn't been her place to send him away.

But what else could she do?

His expression cautious, Rick put his arm around her and led her over to the sofa, away from the chairs he and Tom had been sitting in when she'd entered the room. How long ago was that now, anyway? Time seemed strange. Confused.

'What happened, honey?' he asked, sitting beside her. 'Tell your old dad.'

Violet frowned, trying to find the right words to explain. In the end, what came out was, 'Did you really ask him to interview you about Jez today?'

'Why, yeah. I did.' Rick's eyebrows lifted with surprise. 'Is that what all this is about? Vi, honey, it was my choice. When you asked me earlier about going on stage this weekend...I wasn't sure what I wanted to do. I figured talking it out some might help. And Tom, well, he's a good guy, right? And since all this will probably end up in the book eventually anyway, I wanted to get it down—how raw it feels right now. In case it helps anyone else going through the same thing.'

In case it helped someone else. Sometimes Violet wondered if her parents thought too much about that and not enough about themselves. But that was who they were and she loved them for it, all the same.

'Are you sure it was a good idea?' she asked. 'I mean, everyone wants that interview, and you don't know what Tom is going to do with it now he's—' She broke off with a sob before she could reach the word *gone*.

Rick tugged her closer and she buried her face in his shoulder. 'Do you want me to get your mum? Or your sisters?'

Violet shook her head against his top. 'No. I just...I just need a few minutes.' A few minutes to let the misery out. To let go of all the hope she'd clung to over the last week or so. The chance that her future might be different to her past.

Uncle Jez had probably had that hope too, and look where it had got him.

That thought set off another wave of tears, and Violet didn't try to fight them. She might be all grown up these days, but sometimes a girl still needed her daddy's shoulder to cry on.

Eventually, though, the sobs faded and her tears dried and she knew her dad was going to want some answers.

'You sent him away,' Rick said. Not a question, not even a judgement. Just an opening, to show he was listening if she wanted to explain.

'I found something out about him,' Violet replied, unsure how much she really wanted him to know. Except this was her dad. He'd been there through everything. He'd understand, right? He'd want his little girl safe and happy. 'I know you thought he was a trustworthy journalist, I know that's why you picked him to write your book. But Dad, he wrote a story once. A story that destroyed a girl's life—just like Nick destroyed mine.'

Rick stilled, his arms securely tucked around her. 'You're sure?'

'Very. He admitted it.' Well, sort of. 'He claimed it wasn't the same but then he would, wouldn't he?'

Rick sighed, deep and heartfelt. 'Then I understand why you did what you did. But Violet, I need you to remember something very important, okay?' He pulled back to stare into her eyes, and Violet gave a small nod. 'Your life wasn't destroyed. Remember that.'

Shame filled Violet's chest. Here she was complaining when Uncle Jez's life was gone for ever. And she'd give anything for him to be caught up in a sex scandal right now, even if it meant the papers dragging up her own sordid story all over again.

'I know. Compared to Uncle Jez—'

'That's not what I mean,' Rick said with a sharp shake of the head. 'Think about it, Violet. You still have your home, your family. They took your confidence, and I'll never forgive them for that. But you're still you. You're still my daughter. And you are still loved.'

Warmth filled her, from the heart outwards. 'I know. And I'm so lucky to have you all. But it felt like…they made me someone I wasn't. So they took away who I really am.'

'But they can't.' Rick tapped her on the forehead with one finger. 'She's still in there. And it looked to me like Tom was helping you remember who she is.'

'I thought so too.' Until she'd found out the truth.

There was a pause, and when Violet looked up she saw her dad had on his thoughtful face. The one that always made her mother nervous.

'How did you find out about it? The story he wrote, I mean?'

Violet grimaced. 'Nick called. Told me I should look into his earlier stories.'

'Nick?' Rick's eyebrows launched upwards. '*The* Nick? And you *listened* to him?'

'I hung up on him,' Violet said. 'But…I was curious.'

'As ever.' Rick sighed. 'Did you talk to Tom about it before you threw him out?'

'A bit. I think he wanted to say more,' she admitted.

'Maybe you should listen.' Rick threw up his hands in pre-emptive defence. 'I'm not standing up for the guy— you get to make your own choices about him, and if you tell me he's not someone we should trust then I'll can the whole book idea altogether. He can publish what he has in interviews, but there's not even enough for a novella there. But Vi, if he matters to you—and I think he does—then you have to hear him out. Don't let someone else's version of who he is make your mind up for you.'

Violet nodded, and Rick bent over to kiss her on the

top of the head before moving towards the door. 'Listen to your old dad, yeah? He's been around awhile and sometimes, just sometimes, he knows what he's talking about.'

'I will,' Violet promised. But she couldn't help but be afraid this might not be one of those times.

'Hey, did you see this?'

Violet looked up from the file in front of her to see Rose in the doorway to the study, holding up a newspaper.

'It's less than twenty-four hours until the Benefit, Rose,' Violet said. 'I don't have time to read the paper.'

'You need to read this one.' Rose slipped into the room, revealing Daisy behind her. Daisy took the visitor's chair, rubbing her baby bump, while Rose perched on the edge of the desk, holding out the paper.

Violet sighed. Apparently she wasn't getting out of this without reading something. 'What is it?' she asked, reluctantly reaching out for the paper.

'Tom's first article from his interviews with Dad,' Daisy said, and Violet froze, her fingers brushing the edge of the newsprint.

'You really do need to read it,' Rose added.

God, but she didn't want to. One way or another, this would settle it. If he'd written the sort of story she expected him to, then there'd be no point listening to his side of the story about anything. It really would be over.

And if he hadn't…if by any chance he'd written the sort of story she'd want to read…what would she do then? Risk giving him a second chance?

She wasn't sure she could.

Swallowing, Violet took the newspaper from her sister's hand and skimmed over the section she'd folded it over to. Then, letting out a breath, she read it over again, slower this time.

'It's good, isn't it,' Daisy said after a moment. 'I mean, the guy can really write.'

'Sensitive, too,' Rose added. 'He really got Dad. I've never read an interview with him that made me feel like I was actually there talking with him before.'

'Vi, are you sure…?' Daisy trailed off as Violet shot a glare at her.

She really didn't want to talk about this. On the one hand, she should have known better than to get involved with a reporter in the first place. And if he really, truly did turn out to be a different breed, the lesser spotted good guy journalist…what did it matter now anyway? He was gone. She'd sent him away, and for good reason.

'Did you hear who he got to stand in for Uncle Jez tonight, by the way?' Rose asked. 'God only knows how. I tried to get the band to play second billing to the Lemons when we first put together the programme, but their schedule was crammed. Tom must have really pulled some strings.'

'I'm organising the concert, Rose. Of course I heard,' Violet snapped, then sighed. 'Sorry. I know. He's been great. Right from the start.'

'And yet…' Daisy prompted.

Violet dropped the paper to the desk. If there was anyone she could talk to, anyone who could tell her what she should do next, surely it would be her sisters. Especially since *they* at least seemed to have love all sussed out.

'Have Will or Seb ever done anything, like, in their past? Something you're not sure you could ever understand? Or forgive?'

Rose laughed. 'Vi, honey, Will left four women at the altar, remember? You're his best friend; you know he's not perfect. And was I damn afraid he might do the same thing to me? Of course I was.'

'But you married him anyway,' Violet said.

Rose shrugged. 'It's like Mum and Dad always say. When you know, you know. Will is the one for me. Once I accepted that…everything got a hell of a lot easier.'

Violet turned to Daisy. 'What about you?'

'I thought my marriage could only ever be a show, a business deal,' Daisy reminded her. 'But Rose is right— when you know, you know. So, the question is—do you know?'

Did she? Violet wasn't even sure. 'All I know is that it hurts, not having him here,' she admitted.

Rose and Daisy exchanged a look. Violet wasn't used to being on the outside of those looks. She didn't like it.

'Hurts like a dull ache, like something's missing but you can still feel it?' Rose asked. 'Like a phantom limb?'

'Or hurts like a sharp, blinding pain. The sort that consumes you until you can't think about anything else?' Daisy added.

'Both,' Violet admitted. 'And all the time.'

Rose and Daisy grinned across at each other.

'Honey, you totally know,' Rose said as she hopped off the desk.

'Where are you going?' Violet asked, standing when Daisy stood to follow.

Daisy flashed a smile back over her shoulder. 'To look at maternity bridesmaid dresses, of course. In lavender.'

Violet sank back down into her chair. She wished she could be so confident. Maybe she would have been, before Nick and everything that followed.

She took a deep breath. Maybe she would just have to be again; maybe she could find that lost confidence—if it meant winning Tom back.

He shouldn't be here. Tom was almost one hundred per cent certain he shouldn't be here. But Rick had called and said he was playing after all, and did Tom have any suggestions for a one-off stand-in guitarist for the night…and Tom couldn't not help. Not when he knew what a difference it could make to the night he and Violet had worked so hard to put together.

Even if she didn't want him there.

'Thanks again for doing this,' he said to Owain as a wide-eyed volunteer let them through the artists' gate.

'Are you kidding? Playing with the Lemons? It's an honour, man.' Owain's smile was wide, genuine—and world-famous. Tom had met the guitarist when his band was just starting out, and he'd rapidly become one of those friends he could call on for a night out whenever they were in the same city. These days, Owain's band played sold-out arena tours and, while the frontman might be the most famous member, any true music lover knew it was Owain's guitar playing that made their songs so memorable.

It didn't hurt that he had legions of female fans either, Tom thought. That had to be a bonus for tonight.

'I guess this is where I leave you,' he said as Owain headed through to the bands area. Normally, Tom would have been in there too, mingling, chatting, lining up interviews and soaking in the atmosphere. Tonight, he couldn't take the chance of bumping into Violet.

She had to be around here somewhere, he thought, as he waved goodbye to Owain. Probably racing around, double-checking everything, keeping everything under control in a way he couldn't have imagined her doing when they'd first met.

Strange to remember how he'd thought she was a spoilt rich kid, incapable of doing anything except trade on her parents' names and her own notoriety. He was happy to admit he'd been totally wrong about her.

He just wished she'd believe she was wrong about him, too.

'Tom! You made it.' Rick Cross clapped a hand on his shoulder and Tom tried not to jump.

'Hey. Things going well?' Tom asked, since he couldn't exactly ask, *How's Violet? Where is she? Will she ever forgive me?*

'Best Benefit Concert ever,' Rick announced, then lowered his voice. 'Don't tell Rose I said that, though, yeah?'

'Wouldn't dream of it.'

'Speaking of my girls, have you seen any of them yet?' Rick asked, his tone far too nonchalant. 'Say, Violet, for instance?'

'Ah, no. I thought it was probably best if I stayed out of the way a bit tonight,' Tom said. 'I really just came to bring Owain as a favour to a mate.'

'I see.' Rick subjected him to a long assessing look. 'And here I was thinking that you were here to set things right between the two of you. Never figured you for someone who'd quit at the first hurdle.'

'I'm not…I never said I'd quit.' Tom *wasn't* a quitter. But he also knew when he wasn't wanted. 'Maybe I'm just giving Violet a little space before I make my move.'

'Or maybe you're too scared she'll never trust you.'

How did the old man do that? See right to the heart of his every worry? Tom could understand it working with his daughters, but he'd only known the man a month.

Rick flashed him a quick grin and gripped his shoulder again. 'Don't worry, son. I'm not a mind-reader. But I've been where you are. Sherry and I always say "when you know, you know" and it's true. But we got married in a hurry, and knowing it's the real thing doesn't always make it any easier when times are hard. It just means you know it's worth fighting through.'

'And fighting for,' Tom murmured, almost to himself.

'Always that,' Rick agreed. 'Go on. Go find her. I think she's backstage.'

He shouldn't. This was her big night. She'd worked damn hard for it, and he didn't want to get in her way now. But on the other hand…how could he let this awful feeling in his chest that had started the moment he'd left Huntingdon Hall grow any bigger?

'Backstage, you say.' Tom squared his shoulders, wishing this didn't feel so much like heading into battle. 'Then I guess that's where I'm going.'

CHAPTER TWENTY-ONE

THE ATMOSPHERE BACKSTAGE was incredible. How had she never experienced this before? Normally at the Benefit it would be Rose rushing about behind the scenes, while Violet, Daisy and their mum would watch from a carefully sectioned off area of the crowd.

But now Violet knew—backstage was the place to be.

The act on stage finished their last song with a resounding chord that echoed off the trees surrounding the concert area, and the audience exploded into wild applause. Violet grinned and clapped along as the band traipsed off, high-fiving each other as they came.

'Great job, guys,' she told them, and got wide smiles in return. This was what all the work had been for. To put together a spectacular night that would help raise money and awareness for a cause that really counted.

It almost didn't matter that the person she wanted to share it with wasn't there.

Almost.

'Violet?'

Her breath caught in her throat at the sound of Tom's voice behind her. Of course he was here. How could a music journo miss a night like tonight?

She turned slowly, barely registering the next act as they took to the stage, even as the singer, Sammy, called back to her, something about a shout-out. There was cheering and music and noise all around her, and all she could see or hear was Tom, standing there, solemn-faced, watching her, waiting for her to speak.

And suddenly she had to figure out what she wanted to say.

She'd thought she would have more time. That she could tackle this at her own leisurely pace. But, instead, here he was and she needed to fix things. Somehow.

This could be her last chance.

'Tom.' His name was a start, right? A very small one, but still.

He stepped closer, just one pace. 'Things seem to be going great tonight.'

'They really are.' She bit her lip. 'I wasn't sure if you'd come.'

'Neither was I. But Owain asked me to come with him.'

'That's the only reason?' She almost didn't want to ask. Just in case.

'No.' How could one word send such a flood of relief through her system?

'I'm glad you came,' Violet admitted. 'I wanted to...I never gave you a chance to explain, last time. And I think...I'll listen now. If you still want to talk.'

'I do,' Tom said, but the hesitation in his voice made Violet nervous.

'But?'

Tom shook his head. 'You have a lot going on here today. It can wait.'

'I'm not sure it can.' Violet frowned. There was something more here. Something she wasn't getting. 'What is it?'

Tom leant back against the side of the stage with a sigh, and Violet had to step closer to even hear him over the noise of the band starting up. 'I can explain everything, and I think I can probably do it well enough to make you forgive me. This time.'

'Well, good?'

'But the thing is, Violet, that's only good for this time. What happens the next time I do something you don't agree with, or the next time something reminds you that I'm a hated journalist. You kick me out without listening again?'

'So…you're saying it's not worth trying?' Her stomach dropped lower and lower as every second passed without Tom's answer.

'I'm saying it's something I want you to think about. I want to know that you can trust me because I'm *me*. Not because I can tell you that my editor got a tip from an anonymous source and those photos in a brown envelope, and gave me the story to write as a test. To prove I could. To earn my stripes. And I thought it was just a practice run, that it wouldn't go to print. I don't want you to trust me just because I swear to you I asked him not to print it, and he laughed at me and I realised Mom was right all along.' He sighed, running a hand through his hair. 'I can explain as much as you want, Vi, and I will, probably often if we decide to make a go of things. But I need to know you trust me enough to not *need* the explanation to keep loving me. Does that make sense?'

It did. It was just an awfully big ask.

She opened her mouth to respond, to promise him whatever he wanted if he'd just *stay* long enough for them to sort things out. But then she heard her name blaring out of the speakers on stage, via Sammy, the lead singer's, microphone.

'And a huge shout-out to Violet Huntingdon Cross for putting together such an epic party! Come on out here, Violet!'

'You should go,' Tom said, stepping back from her. 'I don't think she's used to being kept waiting.'

'But we need to—'

'I'll find you later,' Tom said. 'We'll talk then.'

But later would be too late; Violet knew it in her bones. Which meant it would have to be this way, instead. 'Go find Mum and Daisy and Rose. They're out front.'

Tom nodded, and was gone before Violet even stepped out onto the stage.

The lights flashed and burned her eyes and the cheers made her head pound, but nothing could dim her determination. She knew what she needed to do now. She just needed the courage to go through with it.

'Thanks, Sammy,' she said, stepping up to the microphone. She couldn't make out anything beyond the blurs of light in the crowd; she just had to trust that Tom was out there, listening. 'And thank you all for coming tonight.' She paused while the crowd cheered, and tried to ignore the way her knees were shaking. 'The Huntingdon Hall Benefit Concert is always a highlight of the year, but this is the first time I've been able to be so involved in it. You might have noticed that I've been keeping a bit of a low profile over the past few years. But that's...' she stumbled over her words for a moment and bit the inside of her cheek hard, determined to keep it together '...that's going to change.'

There were murmurs running through the crowd now, questions and speculations and probably a few off-colour jokes, too. Violet ignored all of them, looked up into the lights and said what she needed to say.

'I wanted tonight to be a memorial for my Uncle Jez, for his life, and a way of raising both money and awareness for people who find themselves in the same position and need our help.' She took a breath, drawing in courage.

'Whenever we suffer a loss—from a loss of a job, or our reputation, all the way up to a beloved family member—we have to grieve. We have to heal and we have to move on. And sometimes that can be the hardest part—letting go of the past and opening ourselves up to the possibilities of the future. It's taken me a while, but I'm finally able to do that. I am moving on. And you're going to be seeing more of me because of it. I'm going to be out there, raising awareness everywhere I can. I want to let people know that if they need help, it is out there for them. And I want to make sure they get it—because if I can spare one other family a loss like we've suffered this week, it will be worth every minute.'

The roar of the crowd's applause rumbled in her ears and the heat in her cheeks started to fade. She'd done it. She'd taken that step forward and moved on—she just hoped that Tom had seen it.

Because now she needed to find him for the next part.

Handing the microphone back to Sammy, she rushed off stage as the band started up their next song. Weaving her way through the business backstage, smiling vaguely at every clap on the back or supportive comment, she headed for where she hoped Tom would be—with her family.

The pride in his chest felt too big for his body, as if it might burst out of him at any moment. Never mind talking to the press on the phone or holding meetings with managers. Violet had put herself back out there—completely. She'd stood up in front of the crowd, the press and everyone watching on TV and declared herself part of the world again. A woman with a mission.

She wasn't ashamed any more, and it was beautiful.

'Did you *see* that?' Rose bounced up next to him, pure delight shining from her face.

'She was magnificent!' Daisy agreed.

'She most certainly was,' Sherry said, smiling with pride.

'Where is she?' Rose asked. 'I need to hug her.'

'Not until I do,' Tom murmured, and the three women turned to look at him.

Which was, of course, when Violet bounded in.

'Vi! You were brilliant!' Rose and Daisy reached for their sister, and Violet grinned—but her gaze was fixed on Tom's face. He could feel it, even as he stared back.

'Sorry, guys, but I need to talk to Tom,' Violet said.

They both ignored the knowing looks her family exchanged as they headed out of the private area, past the edge of the crowd and around through some of the smaller stalls set up on the outskirts of the concert. Tom vaguely recognised some of the women from the village manning one of the charity support stalls. As they passed them, Violet waved, then reached out to hold Tom's hand. Another sign she was done worrying about what others thought? He hoped so.

Of course, right now he was more interested in finding out exactly what *she* thought about their potential future together.

Eventually, they reached the security barriers out of the concert site, and Violet slipped them through with her pass. 'Where are we going?' Tom asked.

Violet shrugged. 'It doesn't really matter. I just…some things are still private, right?' She flashed him a quick smile and tugged him further along, until they were surrounded by trees at the edge of the wood. 'This will do.'

Tom wanted to ask what, exactly, it would do for. But Violet seemed nervous enough. For once, he'd have to curb his natural impulse to ask questions, lots of them, and let her talk in her own time.

Sometimes, he'd learnt, you got the best interviews that way.

Violet sucked in a deep breath, then let it out again. Tom stamped down on the impatience rising inside him. He had to let her take her time.

'Okay, so…I learnt something while you were gone. Or realised something, I guess. That…maybe people have never been able to move past my past, so to speak, because I've never done anything else. I need to replace those memories—those stories and those jokes—with new and better ones.'

'And that's what you were doing up there on the stage,' Tom guessed.

Violet nodded. 'Starting to, anyway. And it means moving on. Not just from that stupid sex tape, but from the last eight years of hiding, too. Of not trusting anyone and always expecting the worst.'

'Well…good.' Because that sounded positive. But he still needed to hear her say the words.

Violet looked up and met his gaze, her eyes wide and blue and totally open for the first time since he'd met her. 'My mum and dad, they always say that when you know, you know. And I think they're right.' The side of her mouth twisted up into a half smile. 'And I *did* know, deep down. It was just hard to see, behind all that doubt and fear and mistrust.'

'And now?' Tom asked, his heart thumping too hard, too loud in his chest.

'And being without you…it swept all that away. It hurt so much to be apart from you that none of the rest of it mattered any more. All that mattered was telling you that I love you. And I trust you. I do.'

'Really?' God, why couldn't he just take her words at face value?

Violet took his hand between hers. 'Enough to trust you with the rest of my life. If you'll have me.'

Tom blinked. 'You want to get married?'

Violet smiled, slow and warm. 'Why not? It seems to be all the rage this year. Besides, when you know, you know.' She reached up and kissed him once on the lips. 'And I know that whatever happens, whatever you've done or whatever you will do, I trust you to do it for us, not just for a quick story. I'm not the same person I was when that sex tape was made, and I know you're not the same person who let his editor use that story. And I'm not interested in who we were. Only who we can be together.'

And that was all he needed to know. Wrapping his arms tight around her waist, he pulled Violet close, kissing her long and deep until the sounds of the concert, the lights, even the breeze through the trees ceased to register. All that mattered was him and Violet, and their future together.

Finally, he pulled back, just enough to rest his forehead against hers. 'You did the same for me, you know,' he whispered fiercely. 'I spent so many years carrying around the guilt from that story, from my mom never knowing that I realised she was right, even if it was a little late. Meeting you…it made me face that guilt, and all my preconceptions about who you were. If you hadn't shown me that it was possible to move beyond our own pasts…I never could have come back here today. I never could have told you I love you too.'

Violet kissed him again, swift and sharp and full of feeling. But Tom wasn't done talking.

'I should get down on one knee, I know, but I don't want to move that far away from you,' he said, and Violet laughed. 'Violet Huntingdon-Cross. Will you do me the honour of becoming my wife?'

'Only if you'll do me the honour of being my husband,' Violet said, and kissed him again.

'Then it's settled. Your mum gets to plan another wedding.' He squeezed her tighter. 'What do you think? Next summer? Big celebrity bash?'

Violet laughed. 'Haven't you heard? The Huntingdon-Cross sisters don't wait that long for their happy ever afters.'

'True.' Tom smiled. 'Next month, then?'

'Sounds perfect,' Violet said. 'I'm ready to start our new lives. Together.'

EPILOGUE

THE SUMMER SUN shone down on Huntingdon Hall as crowds gathered for the fourth, and final, Huntingdon-Cross wedding celebration of the year. Violet peeked through the curtains of her bedroom, careful not to be seen, and watched the cars pulling up on the long driveway.

Somewhere out there, probably pacing with his soon-to-be brothers-in-law at his side, was her fiancé. She wondered what Tom was making of being the centre of attention for once, instead of just writing about other people's fame.

'Are you ready?' At the sound of her twin's voice, Violet let the curtain fall back into place and turned to smile at Rose.

'More ready than I thought I could ever be,' Violet said.

Stepping forward, the lavender silk of her bridesmaid's dress rustling around her, Rose hugged her sister, a feeling so warm and familiar that Violet felt love in every squeeze.

'Mum is downstairs, waiting to give final approval on the three of us before she heads out to the ceremony area,' Daisy said, her seven-months-pregnant bump appearing a moment before the rest of her came through the door. 'And Dad's just putting the finishing touches to his speech. Again.'

'"Final approval"?' Violet asked with a smile. 'Is she

worried Daisy might get jam on her dress, like she did when she was bridesmaid at Uncle Jez's second wedding?' The pang of pain at the thought of Jez was still there, but already it felt more like a loving memory than a searing loss. The hole he'd left would always be there, but they'd learn to live with it, Violet knew, to move on and make his death meaningful, at least.

'I was five!' Daisy pointed out indignantly.

'Just think, soon it will be your little bump trailing down the aisle in jam-smeared taffeta, leaving rose petals in her wake,' Rose said.

'Well, as long as it's not me, for once,' Violet said, checking her reflection one last time before they headed downstairs. 'I'm done being a bridesmaid, I think.'

'And today you're the bride.' Daisy's words came out a little watery, and Rose handed her a tissue for the inevitable tears.

'Don't start yet,' Rose said. 'We've got the whole ceremony to get through!'

'Not to mention Dad's speech,' Violet added. She wasn't sure if she was dreading or looking forward to hearing which tales of her life Rick Cross thought appropriate to share with the assembled company.

'Can't help it,' Daisy sniffed. 'Hormones.'

'Yeah, yeah,' Rose replied. 'A convenient excuse. They don't seem to be slowing you down any, though, do they? Seb was telling me all about your plans for Hawkesley Castle and his new TV series at dinner last night. It would be nauseating how much that man dotes on you if it wasn't so well deserved.'

Daisy elbowed Rose in the ribs. 'Don't tell me you didn't shed a tear or two when you were making those gorgeous rings for Violet and Tom.'

'Maybe just one,' Rose admitted. 'And they are very pretty, aren't they?'

'They're perfect,' Violet said. 'Just like everything else about today. Now, come on, let's go present ourselves for inspection.'

Violet followed her sisters out of the room, pausing to shut the door behind her. Strange to think she was leaving this place as herself, but would be returning as a married woman. Almost as impossible to believe as the thought of her getting married at all.

But here she was, with her sisters at her side, preparing to say *I do* to the last man she'd ever imagined marrying. And she couldn't be happier.

Sherry Huntingdon-Cross clapped her hands together with delight at the sight of them. 'Oh, don't you all look perfect,' she gushed before wedding planner mode took over again. 'Right, I'm going to head down and take my seat—that's the sign for the ushers to get everyone else seated. Rose, Daisy, you follow just behind me. Then Rick—where is your father, anyway?'

'Here, honey.' Rick Cross came rushing out of his studio, shoving pieces of paper into his pocket. 'Just a couple of last-minute edits. Don't worry,' he added with a wink at Violet. 'I kept the story about that time you fell in the pond at that hotel roof garden when we were on tour in Europe.'

'Oh, good,' Violet said unconvincingly.

'Right,' Sherry said again, commanding everyone's attention. 'I'm leaving. Daisy, Rose, prepare to follow.'

The wedding procession had been timed to perfection. As her father took her arm and led her out of the front door of her childhood home behind her sisters, Violet took a deep breath and followed her family down to the shady clearing, just behind the trees, where they'd set up the chairs and ceremony area. It wasn't a huge wedding—

despite Sherry's attempts—but neither was it the tiny one Violet would have insisted on even a few months ago.

She wasn't scared to share her new happiness, to let others see her moving on with her life in exciting new directions. She wasn't hiding any more.

At the front of the aisle, Tom turned, as if sensing her presence, and Violet couldn't hold back her smile at the sight of him in his perfect suit, waiting for her to join him.

'You ready for this, honey?' Rick asked as the string quartet struck up the canon.

'How could I not be?' Violet whispered back. 'After all, when you know, you know.'

* * * * *

MILLS & BOON®
Hardback – June 2015

ROMANCE

MILLS & BOON®
Large Print – June 2015

ROMANCE

The Redemption of Darius Sterne	Carole Mortimer
The Sultan's Harem Bride	Annie West
Playing by the Greek's Rules	Sarah Morgan
Innocent in His Diamonds	Maya Blake
To Wear His Ring Again	Chantelle Shaw
The Man to Be Reckoned With	Tara Pammi
Claimed by the Sheikh	Rachael Thomas
Her Brooding Italian Boss	Susan Meier
The Heiress's Secret Baby	Jessica Gilmore
A Pregnancy, a Party & a Proposal	Teresa Carpenter
Best Friend to Wife and Mother?	Caroline Anderson

HISTORICAL

The Lost Gentleman	Margaret McPhee
Breaking the Rake's Rules	Bronwyn Scott
Secrets Behind Locked Doors	Laura Martin
Taming His Viking Woman	Michelle Styles
The Knight's Broken Promise	Nicole Locke

MEDICAL

Midwife's Christmas Proposal	Fiona McArthur
Midwife's Mistletoe Baby	Fiona McArthur
A Baby on Her Christmas List	Louisa George
A Family This Christmas	Sue MacKay
Falling for Dr December	Susanne Hampton
Snowbound with the Surgeon	Annie Claydon

GEN STD LP

MILLS & BOON®
Hardback – July 2015

ROMANCE

The Ruthless Greek's Return	Sharon Kendrick
Bound by the Billionaire's Baby	Cathy Williams
Married for Amari's Heir	Maisey Yates
A Taste of Sin	Maggie Cox
Sicilian's Shock Proposal	Carol Marinelli
Vows Made in Secret	Louise Fuller
The Sheikh's Wedding Contract	Andie Brock
Tycoon's Delicious Debt	Susanna Carr
A Bride for the Italian Boss	Susan Meier
The Millionaire's True Worth	Rebecca Winters
The Earl's Convenient Wife	Marion Lennox
Vettori's Damsel in Distress	Liz Fielding
Unlocking Her Surgeon's Heart	Fiona Lowe
Her Playboy's Secret	Tina Beckett
The Doctor She Left Behind	Scarlet Wilson
Taming Her Navy Doc	Amy Ruttan
A Promise...to a Proposal?	Kate Hardy
Her Family for Keeps	Molly Evans
Seduced by the Spare Heir	Andrea Laurence
A Royal Amnesia Scandal	Jules Bennett

MILLS & BOON®
Large Print – July 2015

ROMANCE

The Taming of Xander Sterne	Carole Mortimer
In the Brazilian's Debt	Susan Stephens
At the Count's Bidding	Caitlin Crews
The Sheikh's Sinful Seduction	Dani Collins
The Real Romero	Cathy Williams
His Defiant Desert Queen	Jane Porter
Prince Nadir's Secret Heir	Michelle Conder
The Renegade Billionaire	Rebecca Winters
The Playboy of Rome	Jennifer Faye
Reunited with Her Italian Ex	Lucy Gordon
Her Knight in the Outback	Nikki Logan

HISTORICAL

The Soldier's Dark Secret	Marguerite Kaye
Reunited with the Major	Anne Herries
The Rake to Rescue Her	Julia Justiss
Lord Gawain's Forbidden Mistress	Carol Townend
A Debt Paid in Marriage	Georgie Lee

MEDICAL

How to Find a Man in Five Dates	Tina Beckett
Breaking Her No-Dating Rule	Amalie Berlin
It Happened One Night Shift	Amy Andrews
Tamed by Her Army Doc's Touch	Lucy Ryder
A Child to Bind Them	Lucy Clark
The Baby That Changed Her Life	Louisa Heaton

MILLS & BOON®

Why shop at millsandboon.co.uk?

Each year, thousands of romance readers find their perfect read at millsandboon.co.uk. That's because we're passionate about bringing you the very best romantic fiction. Here are some of the advantages of shopping at www.millsandboon.co.uk:

* **Get new books first**—you'll be able to buy your favourite books one month before they hit the shops

* **Get exclusive discounts**—you'll also be able to buy our specially created monthly collections, with up to 50% off the RRP

* **Find your favourite authors**—latest news, interviews and new releases for all your favourite authors and series on our website, plus ideas for what to try next

* **Join in**—once you've bought your favourite books, don't forget to register with us to rate, review and join in the discussions

Visit **www.millsandboon.co.uk**
for all this and more today!